'You don't have a very high opinion of people, do you?'

'It strikes me, Sandra, that you have the low opinion...of *me*. Is it my wealth, or is it me personally?'

'You can't deny that your image in the media is not a—a commendable one. But I hardly know you—why should you care what *I* think of you?'

'Oh, but I do.' His eyes glinted seductively. 'I do...'

Elizabeth Duke was brought up in the foothills of Adelaide, South Australia, but has lived in Melbourne ever since her marriage to husband John. She trained as a librarian and has worked in various libraries over the years. These days she only works one day a week, as a medical librarian, which gives her time to do what she loves doing most—writing. She also enjoys researching her books and travelling with her husband in Australia and overseas. Their two grown-up children are now married.

Recent titles by the same author:

MAKE-BELIEVE FAMILY
TO CATCH A PLAYBOY

HEARTLESS STRANGER

BY
ELIZABETH DUKE

MILLS & BOON

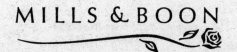

All the characters in this book have no existence outside the imagination of the author, and have no relation whatsoever to anyone bearing the same name or names. They are not even distantly inspired by any individual known or unknown to the author, and all the incidents are pure invention.

*MILLS & BOON and the Rose Device
are trademarks of the publisher.
Harlequin Mills & Boon Limited,
Eton House, 18-24 Paradise Road, Richmond, Surrey TW9 1SR*

© Elizabeth Duke 1996

ISBN 0 263 79430 X

*Set in Times Roman 10 on 11 pt.
01-9603-63503 C1*

Made and printed in Great Britain

CHAPTER ONE

TRENT CORBIN'S silver-grey eyes glittered with the light of battle as his black Mercedes swept up the final slope before the long downward sweep into Kaoga Bay.

Only minutes now to the headland. Corbin land... or it would be soon. All his. Only one man was stopping him now.

The ocean lay to his left, beyond the curtain of eucalypts, the sea an intense blue in the May sunshine. There was no doubt about it—this quiet section of the New South Wales coastline was an untapped gold-mine. If he could only get his tourist resort off the ground and lure more people to come here... Damn it, the place was half dead. It needed waking up a bit.

He let out a muffled oath as an oncoming truck roared over the brow of the hill, forcing him to swerve into the rutted edge of the road.

'Take up the whole road, why don't you?' he bellowed, scowling at the driver as the truck roared past. He was still frowning as he swung the Mercedes back on to the road and swept over the hill.

Too late he saw the cyclist in his path.

Slamming on the brakes, he yanked the wheel round in a last-ditch effort to avoid hitting the bike full-on. A second before the car nicked the packed pannier attached to the rear wheel, he saw the cyclist's head whip round, had a fleeting glimpse of eyes widening in horror under the head-hugging white helmet. Then the bike was spinning off the road into a ditch, its rider landing in a heap of tangled arms and legs in the tufty dry grass.

5

Trent swore. He swung the car off the road and was out almost before he'd brought it to a stop.

The cyclist was lying face down in the grass, not moving.

'Hell, I've killed him!' Trent groaned, only to quench, quickly and coldly, the prickling sensation of dread that rose at the same time, the way he quenched any weakness he perceived in himself. Going weak at the knees wasn't going to help.

Cursing all cyclists, he stooped over the limp figure. The muted earthy colours of the cyclist's drill shirt, knee-length shorts and long thick socks merged into the brown grass. The cyclist's white helmet, however, gleamed like a beacon in the sunlight. It was still firmly in place, Trent noted, so hopefully no serious damage had been done.

Sliding one arm beneath the cyclist's head, he began to remove the helmet carefully. The limp figure stirred, and groaned. Trent hissed out his breath in relief. The lad was only stunned! As he gently eased off the helmet, two things happened simultaneously: a tumble of silky golden hair spilt over his fingers, and a pair of the bluest eyes he had ever seen, unusually long and almond-shaped, looked up at him.

Trent felt something wrench inside him.

'You're a girl,' was all he could say, but already an icy coldness was closing over his heart, bringing a granite-hardness to his strong-jawed face.

The girl sat up, wriggling out of his arms, shaking off his hand.

'And you're a maniac—speeding like that over the brow of a hill!'

She was all right, obviously! 'I was well within the country speed limit,' he bit back, with visions of a tedious court case ahead if he made any rash admissions. 'You were wobbling all over the bloody road.'

He sat back on his heels and blew out a sigh. Why was he snapping her head off? She was probably suffering from shock, and possible unseen injuries as well. But, damn it all, he couldn't seem to help himself.

'I wasn't all over the road.' The blue eyes sprayed sparks. 'And I wasn't wobbling. You were far too close to the edge when you came over the hill.'

'I concede I was well over to the left, thanks to that truck nearly running me off the road. But if you'd been watching out as you should have been and swung away I would never have hit you.' It was stupid, and he knew it, but some demon was driving him on, driving him to lash out at her.

'You gave me no time to swerve off the road,' was her snappish retort.

'Didn't you hear me coming up behind you?'

'How could I with the din that truck was making? And with *that* on.' She glared at the helmet he'd dropped in the grass.

'And look at what you're wearing,' he said scathingly. 'How the hell was I supposed to see you when you're wearing colours that merge in with the road? I thought cyclists were meant to wear bright colours.'

She heaved a sigh and let her head droop, her silky hair falling over her face. 'I didn't want to draw attention to the fact that I was a female, did I?'

A beam of sunlight caught the top of her head, almost blinding him with a dazzle of gold. His insides jerked. In swift rejection he rasped, 'You succeeded in not drawing attention to yourself at all. You merged in so well that you ceased to exist!'

'Pardon me for being alive!' She tossed back her head, the silky hair rippling with lustrous gold lights.

'I take it you're all right, then?' he asked belatedly and not particularly graciously.

'I'm fine, thank you.' There was dignity in the tilt of her small but very determined chin. Then she caught sight of the mangled remains of her bicycle. 'Oh, *no*! Look what you've done!'

He grimaced as he followed her gaze. Oh, great, he thought. Now she *will* sue me.

'I'll have it repaired for you,' he bit out coldly. 'Or if it's beyond repair I'll buy you a new one.'

She looked up at him. 'You will?'

Again those extraordinary blue eyes threatened his composure... but only for a second.

'I've just said I will,' he said curtly.

She bit her lip. Soft, well-shaped lips, he noted, finding his gaze riveted to them, finding them almost as disturbing as her eyes. Lips, he thought, made for kissing...

Oh, hell! As he blanked out the enticing image in icy self-disgust, he saw the lips moving, forming into words.

'You realise it's a specialist touring bike? I doubt if you'll be likely to find a bicycle shop anywhere around here—certainly not a specialist bike shop.'

'Don't worry, I'll arrange it.' He heard the grating harshness in his voice and tried to moderate it. 'Where are you from? You're obviously not a local.' He indicated the packed pannier fixed to the rear of the twisted bicycle.

'No, I'm from Sydney.' She tried to get up, and sank back with a moan, her face screwed up in pain as she reached down to massage her ankle. 'Darn it! I must have sprained the damned thing! I hope I haven't broken any bones.'

She felt it tentatively all around, through the thick sock. 'It's swollen... but I don't think it's broken. No... I'm sure it's not.'

Curiosity got the better of him. 'You're a nurse?'

She shook her head. 'I've... done some first aid.' She obviously had no intention of enlightening him further. 'Oh, this is simply great!' she moaned. 'No bike, and now this!' Her soft hair slid over her face as she reached down to rub her ankle gently. 'Maybe if I just rest it for a minute...' She sighed in frustration. 'Would you mind...?' She glanced doubtfully up at him through the shiny gold strands.

'Go ahead.' He kept his tone dispassionate as he squatted down beside her. 'You mean to tell me you've ridden all the way down here from Sydney? On your *own*?' Speculation, tinged with disbelief, narrowed his eyes.

'Well,' she shrugged, 'I did catch a train to get out of the central city area. You know what Sydney traffic's like.'

'But still...even from the outskirts it's nearly two hundred kilometres.'

'So? I haven't done it all in a day! I've stayed overnight at caravan parks, and spent some time looking around.'

'And you've struck no trouble?' Why, he wondered, did he have the feeling she was lying to him? Or at least keeping something back? It wasn't her answers so much. More a gut feeling. An atmosphere. And shouldn't she be more deeply tanned after days on the open road?

The small chin lifted. It had an attractive cleft in it, Trent noted. She had an equally attractive jawline, and a throat that made him want to slide his fingers down its silky slenderness. A real beauty, he mused. No wonder she tries to hide behind those baggy, colourless clothes and that head-hugging helmet. But what the hell is she doing down here, out on the open road all alone, miles from her home?

Was she running away from something? Or...somebody?

'I've struck no trouble at all.' A warning light glinted in the girl's eyes as she met his gaze.

'Good for you,' Trent drawled. This girl, he thought, with a reluctant stir of admiration, has pluck. She knows how to look after herself. Or she thinks she does. It might be challenging to find out.

He must have smiled unknowingly, because she tensed, watching him suspiciously, the warning vibes growing stronger.

'A friend was coming with me,' she told him crisply, 'but had to pull out at the last minute. It was a bit late to ask anyone else, and to postpone it would have wasted my holiday leave. I only have three weeks, and I've already used up part of one.'

'Male or female?' he asked idly.

'Sorry?'

'Your friend.'

She flushed. 'Does it matter?' And then, as if deciding that was too provocative a question to throw at an unknown male in a remote place like this, she rapped, 'I don't see that it's any of your business!'

He arched an eyebrow at her. 'Sorry. Just curious.' She's mad at herself for flushing, he thought in secret amusement. Interesting...

'Darn this ankle!' She leaned down to resume her rubbing. 'It's not getting any better. It needs some ice.' She glanced down the hill. 'At least I'm near a town. Kaoga Bay, isn't it? I saw it on my map. Could you drop me off there as you pass through? I intended resting up there anyway for a day or two.'

'Sure. But I'm not passing through. I'm heading there myself.'

'You are?' Her eyes narrowed as she took in his white business shirt and tie. 'I thought it was just a holiday place. You don't look as if you're on holiday.'

'I'm not. I have a house there that I work from when I'm not in Sydney.'

He saw the tip of her tongue flick over the soft lips. At the same time he was conscious of a sudden chill in the air—or did the chill come from her eyes? She doesn't trust me, he thought, amused. Or is she as wary as this with all strangers who offer her a lift in their car?

'Look,' he said, 'I'm not planning to run off with you. I'm heading for my home on the headland on the other side of the town. Cross my heart. I'm using Kaoga Bay as my main base at present. I have plans for the town. For the headland, to be precise.'

The vibes were stronger now. Didn't she believe him? He heaved a sigh. 'Look, if you want proof that I've a house there, I can get my wallet and show you. It's in my coat in the back of the car. The Corbins have owned land in Kaoga Bay for close to a century. I spent all my holidays there as a child. My parents retired there. My father died recently and I've come back to settle things... and deal with a few other matters.'

'The Corbins?' the girl echoed. There was an odd inflexion, a brittleness in her voice. So... she knew the name. His mouth took on a thin, sardonic twist, a mocking light flicking into his eyes.

'Trent Corbin,' he spelt out so that she'd be in no doubt.

Her only reaction this time was the merest flicker in the blue eyes. But her very stillness spoke volumes.

'I see my notoriety has preceded me,' he said drily.

She leaned down to massage her ankle. To avoid his eye? he wondered. 'Most people who live in Sydney know the name Trent Corbin,' she said with an indifferent shrug. 'You only have to pick up a newspaper or watch TV. Your name's always popping up on current-affairs shows... in the business pages... at some function or other.'

There was no expression in her voice... none. Whether she was repulsed, impressed, or simply not interested, she was being careful not to show it.

Her lack of reaction intrigued him. It was unusual. Most people reacted strongly and openly when his name was mentioned. Reactions of hatred, jealousy, suspicion... he was familiar with them all. Even open attack. He thrived on it, relishing a good fight. He was equally familiar with the crawlers and the self-seekers, bowing and scraping to a sickening degree. Few were indifferent.

Was she as indifferent as she made out?

'So...' he put a question mark in his voice '... you're aware of my... business dealings?'

She met him eye to eye. 'I'm aware that you're a big property investor... or developer, or whatever you call yourself. You built the Corbin complex in Sydney, didn't you? Exclusive shops and million-dollar apartments for those who can afford them.'

Ah, he thought, his lip curling, so she's not as indifferent as she's trying to make out. 'You take a keen interest in business matters, Miss...?'

She ignored his invitation to supply her name. 'Only when I'm hit over the head with them,' she flung back. 'The papers are forever slapping you in the eye with Trent Corbin's latest glittering proposal: sketch plans, photographs, whatever.'

'If people didn't want them I wouldn't build them,' he pointed out, cynicism hardening his voice.

'Why don't you build something that people really need, like nursing homes, or shelters for the homeless, or housing estates for the elderly, or——?'

'I do those too,' he cut in, 'only they don't make such a splash in the media.'

'Well...' She paused, then rallied. 'I dare say those things are profitable too.'

He leaned back on his heels. 'Do you have some personal hang-up about property developers, Miss—look, what *is* your name?' he asked irritably. 'Or do you have a hang-up about revealing your name to strangers?'

She glared at him. Even angry, he mused, she was a real stunner. Those blue eyes of hers were dynamite.

'My name's Sandra,' she said, adding after a moment's hesitation, 'Sandra Wyatt.'

'Well, Sandra, *do* you have a hang-up about developers? Or is it monetary success in general?'

'Neither!' she snapped. 'Why should I care if you want to make your money the way you do, regardless of the——?'

'Regardless of... what?' he rasped as she caught back the rest.

'Of who you hurt in the process!' she burst out. 'The people you shove aside when you build your shopping centres and your luxury apartment buildings.'

'It's called progress, Sandra. The people I "shove aside", as you so eloquently put it, are more than adequately compensated.' He heard the cynicism in his voice and made no attempt to tone it down. 'A lot of people are only too happy for a developer to come along and offer them a pot of gold. They'd never get the same price from anyone else.'

'What about the ones who don't *want* to sell?'

'Oh, I've found they can usually be persuaded. Money and greed are powerful persuaders.'

The girl's smooth brow furrowed. 'And what about the ones who *aren't* persuaded by money or greed?'

He jerked a shoulder. 'I've yet to meet one. With some people it takes a little time and patience. Some hold out deliberately for a higher price. But they come round in the end. Sometimes it costs you a bit more than you'd like... but that's the name of the game.'

'There must be some who can't be bought!'

'Oh, most people have their price... or some other chink in their armour. Gentle reasoning sometimes does the trick... explaining the project and what it will mean for the community, appealing to their community spirit... that sort of thing.'

'Gentle reasoning... or threats?' she asked quietly.

'I don't resort to threats, Sandra.'

She arched an eyebrow at him. 'What about the case that was in the papers last year? That poor old man who said you were planning to build your shopping complex regardless of whether he sold his house to you or not? You threatened to build *around* his house...'

'That was a bluff to find out how serious he was about staying put.'

'But he *was* serious. I saw him on TV...'

'It was a masterly performance, granted. A consummate actor. He was also a greedy, stubborn, pig-headed old miser. He knew he was the last one in the entire block to sell and he was holding out deliberately for more money. Lots of it.

'All that business about him wanting to stay in his lifelong home till he died was so much hogwash. He knew it would force us to lift our price. He squeezed every drop out of us that he could. And went away laughing. You've never heard him complaining since, have you?'

'I suppose he felt there was no point.'

'No? The moment we admitted that it *was* only a bluff and told him we'd decided against building the complex after all and would be putting the other properties back on the market, the old miser caved in and agreed to sell to us after all—if, as he put it, our price was right. He got his price—though for far less, as it happens, than we'd expected we'd have to pay. So...' Trent let his mouth spread into a thin-lipped smile '...the last laugh was on him.'

She didn't crack a smile. 'It's people like you,' she breathed, 'who turn other people into greedy opportunists.' The look she gave him was withering. 'What they say about you is true. You're ruthless and callous and completely lacking in any human feeling.'

'That's what business *is*, Sandra.' He kept his voice hard, devoid of expression. 'You don't get anywhere by being weak. Or by letting your feelings interfere.'

'Some high-powered businessmen manage to remain human,' she spat back.

'Oh, I'm still human, Sandra.' His gaze scorched over her.

She flushed scarlet and shifted suddenly, making another scrambling attempt to get up, only to wince in pain as she put pressure on her injured foot.

His hand shot out. 'Please... allow me.' Before she could protest one strong arm was under her knees, the other scooping her up into his arms as effortlessly as if she were a child. 'Do you want me to take you to a doctor?' he asked as he carried her to his car. 'You may need an X-ray.'

She shook her head, her hair tumbling over her face, masking her flushed cheeks. 'I'm sure it's only a sprain,' she mumbled, and he could feel the tension in her body, as if she hated being in his arms... or at least was very conscious of it. As he was, he realised, and hardened his heart at the thought.

But despite his steely effort he was still acutely aware of her warmth, the slender weight of her body, the soft curves in his arms. To hell with it, he thought. Why not enjoy the sensation, the feel of her?

'It just needs some ice and a bandage,' she assured him rather breathlessly. 'You can... drop me off in the town.' She gulped, as if fighting to regain her composure. 'I'll m-manage.'

'Oh, yes?' He gave a rough chuckle. 'How? You can't even walk. If you won't see a doctor, you're coming home with me.'

He expected a howl of protest at that too, but it didn't come.

'Well... maybe just until I can walk again,' she mumbled, with a meekness that seemed oddly out of character, from what he'd observed of her so far. He speared a glance down at her, but the blue eyes were masked by the thick sweep of her lashes and by shining strands of hair, glinting gold in the rays of the sun.

'Are you sure you're all right?' he asked, frowning. Maybe she was in more pain than she was making out. Maybe that was why she had suddenly gone so quiet, so...acquiescent. He was surprised she wanted anything more to do with him after that highly suggestive look he'd given her a moment ago, and in the light of what she obviously thought of him.

Or...he eyed the bright curtain of hair speculatively...did she know exactly what she was getting herself into...and was she feeling the same sense of challenge, the same stir of interest, or chemistry, or whatever it was, that he was feeling himself? The thought brought a prickle of anticipation to the hairs at his nape.

'I'm fine, thank you,' she said in the same demure tone. 'Though I'll be glad to take my shoe off and get that ice on my ankle.'

'Won't be long.' He heard the softness in his voice and grimaced. What was it about this girl that was threatening to seep under his skin, threatening to crack the hard shell he'd forged round his heart, the armour he'd sworn no woman would ever breach again? Was it simply the thrill of the chase?

But he'd known that thrill many times before now and he'd never weakened in any way that mattered, never felt anything more than a fleeting pleasure, quickly satisfied and forgotten.

Was it the thought that he'd finally found a challenge that could well prove worthy of him? Mmm...well, as long as he kept in mind that she was simply that—a challenge—and didn't let the girl get to him...

As they reached the Mercedes he felt her stiffen in his arms. Tossing back her hair, she cast a determined look up at him, daggers glinting in the bright blue depths of her eyes.

'Before I get into your car,' she said, almost spitting the words at him, 'I want you to get one thing straight. I can do without the lecherous looks and the snide remarks...or anything else along those lines...savvy? You may be accustomed to females having palpitations at a sideways glance from you, Trent Corbin, but you won't find your so-called manly spell working any magic on me! So either you promise to cut it out in future or I stay put here until another car comes along.'

He threw back his head with a gravelly chuckle. 'Deal,' he promised without hesitation. 'I'd hate to leave you here with only the flies and the lizards for company. As you've seen, there isn't too much traffic along this road at this time of year. And you might notice it's getting rather late in the day.'

'Then I accept your offer,' she said loftily. 'You can put me down now, thank you. I can get in by myself.'

She tried, only to accept some assistance from him grudgingly. She's a plucky little package, he mused as he buckled her into her seat, noting her clenched mouth and the paleness of her face, her delicately tanned skin stretched tightly over her cheekbones. She's in a hell of a lot of pain and she's not making so much as a squeak.

'My home is yours for as long as you need to stay in Kaoga Bay,' he heard himself offering. An offer he'd made no other woman since... *Hell*, he swore under his breath, a glint of cold steel flashing in his eyes.

He deliberately let icy fingers close over his heart as he swung away to pick up the twisted remains of her bicycle. He might want this girl—damn it, he was still a man, with a man's needs!—but it was no more than that. A physical craving of the flesh that could be satisfied quickly and easily, just like all the others... assuming she was willing to participate. But anything more... No. He was dead to all that. Done with it.

But it didn't mean he couldn't have a bit of fun if the challenge was thrown in his face.

CHAPTER TWO

WHAT an amazing piece of luck, Sandra thought as she settled back in the plush leather seat of the Mercedes, literally bumping into the devil himself! All the way down here she had been racking her brain for ways and means to get close to Trent Corbin without arousing his suspicion, and here she was, heading for his home as his guest!

And so far she had fooled him completely! He believed her story that she was a bicycle-touring fanatic and that she'd ridden her bike all the way from Sydney. He believed that Kaoga Bay was no more to her than a stopover on her ride down the coast. He believed that she only knew about him from the newspapers and TV. It was *perfect*.

She would need to keep her ears and eyes wide open, though, and watch her step. Trent Corbin, from all reports, was devilishly clever. And devilishly cold-blooded and ruthless.

A devil, she mused, with eyes like flint, hard, uncompromising features, and the toughness of steel in his long, muscular frame. Obviously not a man to be trifled with.

Still, so far so good. Luck was with her. Of all the people to run her down in his car! It was worth a mangled bike and a twisted ankle. Of course, she could have been badly injured, or even killed, but luckily that hadn't happened. The sprained ankle, painful as it was, was actually a blessing in disguise...

She stretched out her foot deliberately and sucked in an audibly painful breath as a searing pain shot up her leg.

'Bad, is it?' Trent Corbin asked from beside her.

'Not too bad,' she said, flashing him a brave smile. If she could stretch out her injury for long enough, it would give her a perfect excuse to stay in Kaoga Bay— to stay with *Trent Corbin*—for as long as she needed, without arousing suspicion. Or at least long enough, hopefully, to find a way to help her father in his fight against this man.

She felt a deep quiver of antagonism. Did Trent Corbin have any idea, any idea at all, of the strain, the pressure, he was subjecting her father to? Did he even care?

'Ever been to Kaoga Bay before?' the man beside her asked.

She hesitated, then said, 'I've passed through it a couple of times...just briefly.' She might as well be honest about it, she thought. There just might be someone in the town who recognised her from her brief visits to see her father. Unlikely, but possible.

Nobody down here, least of all Trent Corbin, was likely to connect the name Sandra Wyatt with Harry Shaw's daughter 'Alex'. If her father had mentioned her at all to Trent Corbin, which was highly unlikely, he would have referred to her as Alex, as he had always known her and still called her, despite her telling him that she was known as Sandra these days. She had taken the surname Wyatt from her stepfather, her mother having wasted no time in changing it after she'd remarried.

Born Alexandra, she had been called Sandra ever since her father, Harry Shaw, had walked out on his family when she'd been just two years old, running off with the woman who had eventually become his second wife. Sandra's mother, wanting no reminder of the husband who had walked out on her, had coldly discarded the name Alex, as she had then been known, and brutally cut off all connection with him. He had made it easy

for her by moving to another state and making no claim on the daughter he had left behind.

Within the space of three years her mother had acquired a new husband, a new home, and a new family. And Sandra had a new surname...Wyatt. Harry Shaw had ceased to exist.

Sandra slumped deeper into the seat beside Trent Corbin, lost in her memories.

Unbeknown to her mother, who had refused to talk about Harry, she had always been curious about the father who had abandoned her at such a young age. Having never really grown close to her stepfather or to her two half-brothers, she had left home at the age of seventeen, with the hope of one day tracking Harry down.

Eventually, in the final year of her physiotherapy course in Sydney, she had found out where he was. He was living in Melbourne with his second wife. Still happily married, they'd had no children—the one sadness in their lives. Harry had been stunned and delighted when the daughter who he had long thought was lost to him had written to him asking for a meeting.

The meeting, though difficult and emotional, had healed a lot of the old wounds. Harry had told Sandra that he and her mother had both realised, almost from the start, that their marriage had been a ghastly mistake.

He had walked out after he had fallen deeply in love with the woman who was now his wife, knowing his life would be meaningless without her...a woman closer to his own age than Sandra's mother, who had been much younger. He had bowed to Sandra's mother's demands to keep away from the daughter he adored because he hadn't wanted to cause either of them any more trouble or distress.

Sandra, without expecting to, had found Harry's second wife a charming woman—far warmer and more compassionate than her own mother—but she had felt

like an intruder in their home. The two were so close, and had been on their own for so long, that she'd sensed they didn't need anyone else. It wasn't until Harry's wife had died a few years later that she and Harry had begun to grow closer.

During that time Harry had retired and moved to Kaoga Bay to live with his recently widowed sister-in-law, a semi-invalid, who had needed someone to look after her and her cliff-top property. Sandra had driven down once or twice to visit them, but her busy life at the sports clinic where she'd been working by then as a qualified physiotherapist had kept her from seeing Harry as often as she would have liked.

About eighteen months ago Harry's sister-in-law had died, leaving Harry her cliff-top home. Harry had gone on living there alone, enjoying his life there, fishing, camping, tending his beloved vegetables, or just pottering around his property doing odd jobs.

Although Sandra had only managed a couple of flying visits to Kaoga Bay since Harry had been on his own, and had only been able to lure him to Sydney once to visit her, she and her father had grown closer in the past eighteen months than they had ever been, keeping in regular contact by phone.

But his recent phone calls had been worrying. Old Marshall Corbin, long-time owner of the sprawling cliff-top property adjoining Harry's, had died a few months ago, and since then Trent Corbin, Marshall's only son, had been spending more and more time at Kaoga Bay, 'plotting', as Harry put it, what to do with the old Corbin home and property. He had been gradually buying up all the other houses and properties on the headland, with the idea, Harry had discovered, to his disgust, of building a luxury tourist resort on the headland, overlooking the ocean.

Harry's was the last property remaining unsold. In many ways it was in the most desirable position of the

lot, having not only a spectacular ocean view from the cliffs in front of his house, and views along the coast, but also access to a private cove from the side of his property.

'You're very quiet,' Trent said. 'Are you sure you're OK?'

She started at the sound of his voice. They had already passed through the small seaside town and she had barely noticed. Now they were on the rise again, winding up the headland road through the low scrub and gum trees, with the occasional glimpse of houses through the trees, some already in the throes of being demolished.

'Are we nearly there?' she asked, feigning a wobble in her voice.

'Nearly. We're on Corbin land now. My family have owned a good part of this headland for over a century. All but one of the other properties here now belong to me.' Satisfaction was evident in his voice. 'Very soon, I hope, I'll own this entire headland.'

Not if Harry and I can help it, Sandra vowed silently, her lips tightening to a grim, determined line. Harry was up in arms, and rightly so. He'd mentioned veiled threats. Trent Corbin, not stupid enough to threaten Harry to his face, had sent his burly stand-over man, Roland, to make them for him. Roland, Harry had told her, looked after Corbin's property at Kaoga Bay and kept a watchful eye on his boss's other headland properties.

And it hadn't stopped at threats. Already Harry's property had suffered a bout of vandalism. Sandra had decided it was high time she came down to see what she could do to help her father, eager to support him in his valiant fight against this powerful man.

She hadn't consulted Harry. She could be of more use to her father, she had decided, coming to the bay on the quiet and making a few enquiries for herself first, without anyone knowing who she was. People would be

bound to clam up if they knew she was Harry Shaw's daughter.

From under her fringe of lashes she stole a look at the man at the wheel. 'Corbin land', he had arrogantly called it, as if he had a God-given right to it...and to the entire headland. He was everything she had heard about him: heartless, arrogant and overbearing. A dangerous man to have as an enemy.

Just *how* dangerous she'd had a taste of when he'd swept her up into his arms and carried her to his car. Held so close, she had felt his sexual magnetism, and, worse, had reacted to it. The rub of his fine silk shirt against her cheek, the warmth of his chest through the fine fabric, the play of his muscles as he walked, even the faintly musky scent that clung to him, had had an intoxicating and disturbing effect on her.

The fact that she could react to him at all—*Trent Corbin*, of all men!—frightened and dismayed her.

She gulped and flicked her gaze away. She had been physically attracted to men before, but never this strongly, never in the mindless, irrational way she'd felt just now, with the dizzy feeling that if he'd held her for much longer she could easily have lost control of her mind as well as her body.

In Trent Corbin's powerful arms she had felt a numbing weakness, a loss of power and control that she'd never come close to experiencing before. She had always known in the past exactly what she was doing, at all levels of a relationship, and because she had never lost her head, let alone her heart, she had been able to remain in control, no matter how intimately involved she had been at the time.

The weakness he'd made her feel—coming on top of the lewd look he'd given her a moment earlier—was why she had lashed out at him before she would get into his car. Trent Corbin, for heaven's sake, had to be the last man on earth...!

A sudden gust of wind buffeted the car.

'We get some strong winds up here on the headland,' Trent said. 'But I wouldn't be surprised if this is blowing up into something bigger than normal. Mmm...' he said as the ocean burst into view ahead of them. 'Take a look at those black clouds rolling in from the sea. I reckon we're in for quite a storm.'

Sandra thanked her lucky stars that she wasn't cycling out on the open road now. Who would have believed, looking at that clear blue sky only minutes ago, that black clouds could roll in so ominously fast?

Her eyes strayed to her left, to a small cottage half hidden, at this angle, by clumps of eucalypt and scrubby bush. 'Is that your house over there?' she asked, and turned in all innocence to watch his face as he answered. She tried to hide a surge of angry resentment as she noted the thinning of his lips, the darkening of his brow, the ruthless glow in his eye.

'No. That's the place I was telling you about. The only property I haven't been able to get hold of. Yet.' There was implacable purpose in that clipped 'yet'.

'The family don't want to sell?' With an effort, she kept her tone coolly impassive.

'It's not a family. It's just one stubborn old-timer who was lucky enough to inherit the place from a widowed relative. Not even a blood relative.' He scowled. 'The house is too big for him. The property is beyond him ... you should see the state it's in. And he's not even a genuine local. He's a blow-in from interstate.'

She gulped down her outrage. 'Do only locals have the right to live here?' she demanded. 'I thought Kaoga Bay was a popular place for people to retire to.'

'It is, and I've no objection to that. By all means let them settle in the town or around the beaches. I *want* to attract people here—retirees, tourists, families, the lot. I have great plans to do just that. But Harry Shaw is stopping me. Being stubborn, just for the sake of it.

Kaoga Bay means nothing to him. He has no family background here, no roots to hold him here. He hasn't even been here for long.'

'But if he's happy here——'

'He could be just as happy,' Trent cut in, 'living anywhere along this coast. I've even told him I'll help him find a place. Damn it, he doesn't need to go on living where he is. I have plans for this headland. Big plans. And he's standing in my way!'

Sandra thrust out her jaw. Obviously people stood in Trent Corbin's way at their peril! 'If he's refusing to sell to you, obviously he doesn't agree that he *would* be happier elsewhere!' She clenched her hands into fists as she tried to keep control. It was an effort to speak dispassionately, to keep her anger, her indignation, her resentment from her voice.

'We'll see,' Trent grated. 'I upped my offer a few days ago—to a crazy level that only a fool would knock back. I told Harry to think about it. The stubborn idiot was adamant he would still refuse. I said, So be it—it's my final offer, and walked out.

'I haven't been near him since. I've spent these past few days up in Sydney. With luck my offer will have sunk in by now and he'll be starting to worry that I've lost interest and won't give him another chance to change his mind and sell. A cooling-off period won't do him any harm at all.'

Sandra shivered at the callous self-satisfaction in his voice. He sounded so sure of himself! How much longer could her father hold out against such relentless determination?

'You're cold?' She felt Trent's hand feeling for hers, stroking over it, and she shivered again, this time at his touch.

'A bit.' The temperature inside the car had dropped. But her palms felt hot and clammy. Not wanting him to notice it and wonder why, she pulled her hand out from

under his and folded her arms as if to warm herself, curling her hands underneath, out of his reach.

'Almost there.'

Trent swung the car round to the right, along a gravel track with bush closing in on either side. The sky was getting darker by the minute.

'This is it,' he said a moment later as the Mercedes emerged from the scrub and came to a standstill alongside a solid-looking two-storey house. Through the gloom she took in its pale grey walls, the white-framed windows, the French doors under the columned loggia. An impressive tower rose from the junction of the two hip-roofed wings of the house.

Some holiday house, she thought. Some retirement home.

'Stay put,' Trent commanded, throwing open his door. She watched him stride round to her side of the car, her heart quickening as he opened the door and reached down to help her out. She thought of her father as she felt his hands on her, as she smelt the musky maleness of him, as she felt the warmth of his breath on her face.

'No need to carry me!' she heard herself snapping at him. 'I can hop if you'll just——'

'Don't be a fool. See how black it's getting? It's going to come down in buckets any second.' She was in his arms before she could protest further, his arms bearing her weight as easily if she were a bubble of foam from the sea.

I'm not enjoying this...I hate it—I hate *him*, she thought in agitation, gritting her teeth and tensing her body as he carried her up the front steps, through a wide archway and into the shelter of the tiled loggia. A flash of lightning brought a brief ghostly brightness to the ominous darkness around them.

As a deep rumble of thunder rolled across the sky, the front door of the house burst open and Sandra found herself staring up at a blond-haired giant, his bulging

biceps, skin-tight black T-shirt and equally tight jeans accentuating his hugeness.

She noted that he didn't even blink at the sight of his boss carrying a young woman into his house. Was it a common occurrence? she wondered with a cynical twist of her lips.

'Here, Mr Corbin, let me...'

She felt herself shrinking back against Trent Corbin's chest as the blond giant reached out his burly arms as if about to pluck her from his boss's grasp.

'It's all right, Roland.' Trent swept past him. 'You bring in Miss Wyatt's bags from the car. You'll find them attached to the wreckage of her bicycle in the boot. We had an unfortunate collision coming into the bay. Miss Wyatt has an injury to her ankle.'

'Are *you* all right, Mr Corbin?' Roland asked, his pale, close-set eyes showing swift concern. More concern, Sandra thought wryly, than he was showing for her!

'I had the car to protect me, Roland.' Trent's tone was dry. 'The car may *not* be all right. I haven't checked.'

He hadn't either, Sandra realised in surprise. Most men would have checked their car for damage—if not first up, at least after making sure they hadn't killed or seriously maimed the person they'd hit. In Trent Corbin's case, no doubt he was so well off he didn't need to bother about minor damage bills...

Or hadn't he even thought of checking his car, his concern for *her* driving it out of his mind?

And pigs might fly, she thought derisively.

Roland was already clumping off down the steps, slavish obedience in every line of his huge frame. How, Sandra wondered curiously, had Trent Corbin earned such blind obedience? With money? The sheer force of his personality? By using his tongue to verbally beat the giant into submission?

Whatever means he'd used, Roland didn't seem to resent it. On the contrary, he seemed to lap it up. Did

genuine regard, devotion even, accompany his slavish obedience? she found herself wondering.

'Ah, Magda...' As Trent carried her into a high-ceilinged square vestibule with a richly patterned Persian carpet on the floor and a winding staircase at the rear, a woman appeared, her plump middle-age and the apron she was wearing seeming to indicate that she was Trent's cook or housekeeper.

'We have a house guest,' he told her. 'I'm afraid Miss Wyatt is suffering an injured ankle. The spare room downstairs is made up, is it? Good. We'll need some ice and bandages. And after you've brought us those you could ring Dr Grey. I want him to come and——'

'Please, there's no need,' Sandra protested. 'Let's just try the ice first. I'm sure I'll be fine by morning.'

'While you're under my roof you'll do as I say, all right?' Trent said, his expression brooking no argument. A man used to having people jump at his every command, Sandra gathered, watching in some bemusement as Magda spun away with the same respectful obedience that Roland had shown.

Are they scared of him? she wondered. Trent Corbin, she knew, had a formidable reputation for getting things done, for sweeping problems aside—and people too— to get what he wanted. A man who rode roughshod over anybody who stood in his way.

As Harry stood in his way.

She compressed her lips as Trent carried her past the staircase and along a passage lined with seascapes and a couple of old family portraits. She caught sight of a wall phone as they swept past it. Should she try to ring Harry later and let him know that she was here in Trent Corbin's house? He might want her to keep her eyes and ears open while she was here.

No...perhaps not, she decided. Someone could be listening in on another phone. She would keep her eyes and ears open anyway.

She noted some slips of paper on the small table underneath. Perhaps there was something incriminating there—a number, a name—that Harry could use in his fight against Corbin? Dared she try to glance through them later?

The moment the weather cleared up and she was mobile enough to walk, she would have to find some excuse to leave the house and hobble over to Harry's. A scenic amble around the headland . . . nobody would question that. She would make sure first, of course, that Trent and his henchman Roland were otherwise occupied.

An explosive bang that almost shook the house from its foundations made her jerk convulsively in Trent's arms and fling her arms around his neck. He gave a soft chuckle and tightened his grip on her, cradling her against him in a way that made her cheeks burn. But, much as her mind willed it, her clutching hands wouldn't seem to loosen their grasp from around his neck.

His voice, rumbling just above her right ear, seemed to coil right down to the base of her stomach. 'Just thunder . . . directly over the house, by the sound of it. We get some mighty storms up here on the headland at times.'

The last part was almost drowned out by the thunderous crash of rain on the iron roof, slashing down in a solid, deafening sheet. Sandra stifled a groan. If this kept up for long it would be too wet to venture outside for days!

They reached a partially open door; Trent kicked it wide and carried her in. For a family holiday house, it was a very grand spare bedroom, with dusky pink drapes at the window and dark antique furniture. A deep, rose-coloured carpet muffled Trent's footsteps as he strode across the room to the four-poster double bed and lowered her down on to the soft floral eiderdown.

'Let's get that shoe off first.' He reached down to ease it off her swollen foot.

'Ouch!' Her body arched in a spasm of pain.

'Sorry.' He took more care peeling off her thick sock, glancing up as Magda bustled in, bearing an ice-pack and bandages. No flies on Magda, Sandra thought. When Trent said 'jump', people jumped.

Trent took the ice-pack and laid it gently on her bruised, swollen ankle. 'Thanks, Magda. Now go and make that phone call, will you?'

'I don't need a doctor!' Sandra's sharp voice halted Magda in her tracks. She looked appealingly up at Trent, who was frowning. Obviously, he didn't like his orders being countermanded. 'I do know something about sprains,' she told him steadily. 'I'm quite sure that by morning it will be much better...so long as I keep it up and put ice on it for a while to help the swelling and bruising—and then support it with a firm bandage. A hot pack later might help too.

'I promise if it's any worse in the morning I'll see a doctor then and have X-rays. But I'm quite sure...'

She trailed off as Trent held up a hand to silence her. Turning his head, he waved Magda impatiently from the room.

'You sound as if you know what you're talking about,' he said grudgingly as he turned back to face her. 'All right, we'll leave it till morning, since you're sure it's not broken.'

Afraid that he was going to delve into *how* she was so sure—what if Harry had mentioned to him that he had a daughter who was a physiotherapist and Trent put two and two together?—she said quickly, 'Anyway, it wouldn't be fair to ask anyone to come out in this storm. It's teeming outside.'

As if to add weight to her argument, another explosive clap of thunder rocked the house and the crashing rain reached deafening new heights.

'It's a doctor's job to come out, storm or no storm,' Trent growled with a callous disregard for the man.

Sandra bit back a gasp of anger. No heart at all, she thought. None. Just like people say. She bent her head to hide her reaction from him.

'Ready for your bandage?' Trent asked, hovering over her.

'I can manage,' she mumbled.

'As you like.' He stepped away. 'I'll send Magda back in to unpack your clothes and help you undress. You'll find the bathroom through that door over there. I'll drop my father's walking stick in to help you hobble around.'

'Thank you.'

'Want me to make any phone calls for you?' he asked, pausing at the door. 'Your family? Friends?'

She shook her head. 'No need, thanks. My flatmate's away and,' she improvised quickly, 'it would only alarm my mother if you rang her.' She remembered the papers on his phone table in the hall. 'Um...I might give her a call myself later, if that's OK with you?'

She could pretend to dial her mother's number, and later say there'd been nobody at home. She had no intention of letting her mother know she was here. As far as her family were concerned—and Harry too for that matter—she was spending her holiday break on a cycling tour of the Blue Mountains with her touring club—which she had fully intended to do until Harry had mentioned threats...and the damage to his property. Harry, she had resolved, was far more in need of her support than she was in need of a holiday.

'As you wish.' Trent swung away. 'If you need any more clothes, by the way, you may find something suitable in the wardrobe. My sister left some stuff there and she's about your size.'

'Your sister?' Sandra glanced up at him. 'She comes to stay here too?' She hadn't heard about any sister.

What did *she* think of her brother's plans for the headland?

Trent halted at the door. 'Not any more, no. She lives in London with her husband and family.'

'Oh.' Curiosity—and a dim hope—plucked another question from her. 'She doesn't mind that you're planning to demolish the family home?'

'Why should she? Anyway, she has no say in the matter.'

'She doesn't?' Her heart sank. 'You mean your father left the house to you alone? Your sister didn't even get a half-share?'

She caught her breath at her impudence in asking such an intrusive question, and could have kicked herself when the dark eyebrows slanted in a frown. What business was it of hers? he must be thinking. She hoped he wasn't also wondering *why* she was so interested in the fate of his family home.

His answer was curt. Crushing. 'My sister did get a half-share but I bought her out. She had no further use for it and was grateful for the money.'

Sandra's gaze fluttered away. How much persuasion, she wondered cynically, had it taken to convince his sister? How much money had he been forced to part with? Uncaring, unfeeling monster, she thought contemptuously. Family...family ties, family property...none of those things meant a jot to him. The family home was no more to him than another slick business opportunity.

In her indignation, she threw discretion to the winds. She was darned if she was going to let him off the hook so easily!

Facing him defiantly, she demanded, 'You're saying your sister doesn't care about what you're planning to do with the family home? What if she wants to come back to Kaoga Bay one day for a visit? What if she wants

to bring her family back and show them where she stayed as a child?'

The cold silver eyes met hers unwaveringly. 'What if she does? She can still come to the bay. She can still stay up here on the headland. The resort I have in mind will have all the facilities she could possibly want in a holiday location.'

'But surely staying at the old family home is...different?' she persisted. 'More meaningful. More...personal.' Why was she bothering? Only for Harry's sake! But trying to give Trent Corbin a sense of what it meant to some people to *belong* to a certain place was plainly futile. Nothing would penetrate that unfeeling, bullet-proof hide of his!

His answer confirmed the thought. 'Why should it be?' She had never heard such implacable, dismissive coldness in anybody's voice. 'The bay itself hasn't changed. That's what people come here for—for the beaches, the fishing, the surfing, the views.'

'So you have no sentiment at all about the house, no feeling of...nostalgia.' Her voice was heavy, her heart without hope. It wasn't even a question. She already knew the answer.

'Sentiment and nostalgia are crutches for the weak.' His voice was so hard and pitiless that it made her shiver. She bit back the retort that sprang to her lips. Careful, Sandra! You don't want to alienate him completely...if you haven't already. But, try as she might, she was unable to hide the contempt in her eyes.

He saw it too. She could tell by the way the silver eyes darkened to slate-grey, by the rock-like hardening of his features. When he spoke, his tone was icily abrupt. 'I'll have Magda bring your dinner in on a tray. You'd better stay put for this evening and keep that foot up. Best way to get your ankle back to normal.'

So that he could be rid of her quickly? She nodded meekly, thinking, We'll see about that. I'll be leaving

here, Trent Corbin, when I'm good and ready. And if
that means curbing my tongue a little better, and playing
up to you a little more, than that's what I'll make an
effort to do.

For Harry's sake.

CHAPTER THREE

THE storm was still raging when Magda brought her dinner in on a tray. The woman was guarded and uncommunicative. All she said as she handed over the tray was, 'I hope you like fettucini?'

'It looks delicious.' Sandra smiled up at her.

'I'll come back later for the tray.' Magda stepped away. 'And bring you another ice-pack.'

'Oh, please don't worry, Magda; I can bring the tray back myself. Mr Corbin has brought me a walking stick so that I can hobble around. And instead of ice I think I'll try some heat treatment next, which I can get for myself. I'll just soak a towel in hot water.'

'I'll come back for the tray,' Magda insisted. 'And bring a fresh bandage for your ankle.' Boss's orders, Sandra surmised.

'I'm sorry I'm giving you all this extra trouble, Magda,' she said, her tone sincere.

Magda looked faintly startled, and turned to face her squarely for the first time.

'No trouble,' she said in a softer but still cautious tone.

Sandra smiled, resisting for the time being the temptation to ask the questions she was longing to ask.

Later, when Magda came back with a neatly folded bandage, and reached for the dinner tray, Sandra said warmly, 'That was delicious, Magda. The golden pudding too. Thank you. My mother used to make puddings like that when I lived at home.'

She glanced towards the curtained windows and sighed. 'I hope this storm passes over quickly so I can

get out into the fresh air. Kaoga Bay is such a lovely spot, isn't it? Have you lived here long?'

Magda paused, the tray in her hands. 'I've been with the family since Trent was a boy.'

'Oh, I see.' So she must know Trent well. Was her deference to him born of a wary respect for the boy who had grown into a ruthlessly powerful tycoon... or based on genuine devotion?

'It will be a wrench for you, I imagine,' she said, her tone sympathetic, 'seeing the home you've lived in for so long being demolished to make way for a tourist resort.'

For a brief second Magda's brown eyes wavered under hers. Then they snapped away. 'Mr Corbin has promised to look after me. He'll find me a place I can retire to... where I can live in comfort for the rest of my life. He is a kind and generous man,' she asserted, her tone faintly defiant, as if she knew what people said about him and was anxious to refute it.

Kind? Generous? Sandra tried to fit those qualities to the man who was callously hounding her father, and couldn't. Magda would be seeing him through rose-coloured spectacles, of course, having been with the family for so long.

'Well, it might not even happen yet,' she said carefully. 'If your neighbour refuses to sell his place next door, that is.'

Magda gave her a sharp look, her mouth tightening. 'Harry Shaw is being very stubborn and pigheaded. Mr Corbin has offered him a brand-new home wherever he wants to go.'

'But he doesn't seem to *want* to go...Mr Corbin says.'

'Mr Corbin will talk him round... in the end.'

Will pressure him until he caves in, you mean, Sandra thought, closing her eyes momentarily to hide a flash of resentment.

'Your ankle is hurting?' Magda asked swiftly. 'Let me get a hot towel for it,' she offered, heading for the bathroom. 'You should stay put.'

Sandra leaned back against the pillows. 'Thank you, Magda. You're very kind.'

It was Magda, surprisingly, who brought up Harry's name again when she came back with a heat-soaked towel. 'If I'm prepared to give up the home I've lived in for years,' she muttered primly as she wrapped the towel round Sandra's ankle, 'why shouldn't Harry? He's only been here a short time.'

With an effort Sandra kept her expression bland. 'What's he like?' she asked casually. 'Has he been a good neighbour?'

Magda shrugged. 'We never saw much of him even before all this, though he was friendly enough when we did,' she admitted grudgingly. 'But since Mr Corbin senior died and young Mr Corbin started buying up all the other properties...' Her shoulders lifted and fell, her lips pursing in a grimace.

'It's strained relations...I can imagine,' Sandra said, nodding. 'What a shame.' She sighed. 'Well, as Mr Corbin says, that's progress. I guess I'm a bit of a sentimentalist. I don't like the thought of people losing things that *mean* something to them. This is such a lovely house. And Harry Shaw's cottage next door too—from what I've seen of it,' she hastened to add.

Magda's eyes flickered, showing her surprise, as if she expected that any guest of Trent Corbin's—particularly a woman guest—would be eager to back him unconditionally, not criticise him. Well, Sandra thought in satisfaction, at least Magda will know now that I'm not here to chase after her boss! She might even pass on what I've said to Trent. Like the loyal retainer she is, I'm sure she will!

She sensed that Magda agreed with her, deep down. Would Trent have second thoughts if Magda could con-

vince him that the changes he planned would *hurt* people?

Some hope, she thought in the next breath. Magda wouldn't even try, knowing it would be a pointless exercise, appealing to a man like Trent Corbin, no matter how long she'd known him. It would be pointless to expect a change of mind from that heartless, coldly ambitious money-making machine.

'Mind if I come in?'

They both jumped, almost guiltily, Sandra shooting upright in her bed, Magda springing back, as if dismayed that he had found her still there.

'I've just given Miss Wyatt a hot pack,' she muttered, snatching up the tray and heading for the door.

'Ah ... beat me to it, did you, Magda?' was Trent's benign response. 'I was coming in to offer to do just that. Thank you,' he called after her, and Sandra was surprised—pleasantly surprised—at the mildness of his tone, when she had been expecting mistrust or annoyance at seeing them both so chummy.

She was even more pleasantly surprised to hear him addressing someone with such friendly respect, even warmth, rather in that autocratic, scathing tone she had heard so often on the radio and TV, and had been on the receiving end of herself.

He had changed out of his business suit and tie into a black sweater and thigh-hugging black jeans that made him look even more dangerously attractive. And unnervingly virile.

'Well, you two seem pretty cosy,' he remarked, his eyes narrowing—in wariness or in surprise? 'Magda's a pretty hard nut to crack,' he added, his lip curving a fraction. 'How did you manage it?'

'Manage it?' she echoed. 'I didn't *manage* anything,' she said disparagingly. 'Not everyone's as manipulative and calculating as you!' As the words spilt out she flushed, partly at her rudeness and partly in guilt, be-

cause she *had* gone out of her way to draw the woman out.

A roll of thunder drowned out her mumbled apology. As another sharp deluge followed, she averted her face from his, her thick lashes sweeping down over her flushed cheeks. 'I...' she faltered. 'I'm not myself at the moment. Maybe I'll feel more human in the morning. When this wretched ankle stops hurting.'

He bent over her. 'Is the heat helping?' He sounded almost sympathetic!

'A bit. Thanks.'

He reached down to touch the warm towel with his fingertips. 'Want me to reheat it?'

She flicked her tongue over her lips, very conscious of his feather-like touch—and of his dark, muscular frame bending over her, blotting out the warm glow from the bedside lamp. 'I think I've had enough heat, thanks!' As she leaned down to unwrap the towel from her foot her hand brushed against his, sending a tingling shock through her. 'I'll just bandage it——' she gulped '—and——'

'Allow me.'

'I can——'

'I'll do it! You can instruct, if you think I'm doing it the wrong way.'

She swallowed, holding her breath as he carefully removed the towel and with surprisingly capable fingers began to bind the supporting bandage round her foot and ankle, making it firm but not too tight. Then he gently stroked his hands over it—quite unnecessarily, she thought—as if making sure he had it just right.

'Anything else I can get for you?' He straightened slowly, his voice low and ever so faintly mocking.

She gulped. 'Nothing. Thanks.'

'Then I'll say goodnight. I'll be in my office along the passage if you...need me.' He stood looking down at her, and she was glad that she was lying down as their

eyes clashed and she felt a flare of heat race through her body and down her limbs.

If only she could read what that look of his meant. There were so many flickering lights and veiled emotions in the silver depths that she felt breathless trying to decipher them. But softness and warmth, she was sure, weren't among them.

She managed to unlock her tongue. 'I'll be fine,' she assured him, and heard the huskiness in her voice. She gave a tiny cough to clear it. 'I might slip out in a few minutes and make that phone call...'

'Like any help?' he offered, pausing.

She shook her head. 'It's only a few steps. And I have your stick. Then I'll...try to get some sleep.'

'Well, pleasant dreams, Sandra,' he said, and his eyebrows rose fractionally—as if daring her to dream about him...?

She gave him time to settle down in his office and then rose carefully from the bed and hobbled to the phone in the hall, making sure before picking up the receiver that there was nobody around. The skies shook and rumbled overhead and the rain drummed down on the roof as she dialled the number of her own flat and let it ring and ring, knowing full well that there would be nobody there.

With her other hand she began to leaf idly through the slips of papers on the small table below. There were phone numbers, hastily scrawled notes and a few names jotted down that meant nothing to her. And the names of a couple of prominent charities.

Charities! She frowned. They hardly fitted the image of the devil incarnate! Unless, she thought nastily, Trent was keen to acquire *their* premises and was planning to buy *them* out!

Leaving the slips of papers as she'd found them, she hung up and headed back to her room, limping along

with the aid of the walking stick, the elastic bandage still firmly in place round her ankle, offering good support.

Before she reached the door of her room a voice from behind nearly made her jump out of her skin.

'Did you get hold of your mother?'

She swung round guiltily to see Trent Corbin lolling in the passage, the dim lighting casting his face into deep shadow. She hadn't heard a sound. He must move as silently, as stealthily as a panther! In fact, in his black sweater and jeans, he did look every inch the stalking black panther. And the shadows across his strong face made him look positively satanic!

She made an effort to answer lightly, normally. 'Afraid not. She . . . they must all be out. Now that I think of it, they were talking about going away for a couple of days. They must have gone already.'

She bowed her head as she spoke, and winced, as if to hide a stab of pain, letting her soft hair slide like a curtain over her face. She had an uncomfortable feeling that those piercing grey eyes of his didn't miss much, and she wasn't much good at lying.

'Better get that foot up,' Trent advised, a sardonic note in his voice, almost as if he *knew* she was hiding something from him and was wondering just what.

She drew in a deep breath. Had he been hanging around in the passage for long? The alarming thought that he might have seen her going through his telephone notes sent her heart fluttering to her toes. Was he already suspicious, already wondering why she had agreed so readily to come into his home?

'I must try to get some sleep!' she almost gasped. 'It's been a—a pretty gruelling day!'

'Yes, of course,' he agreed silkily. 'You've ridden all this way . . . all alone.' He glanced down at her bandaged foot. 'And then for this unfortunate thing to happen . . .'

Again she heard it . . . something in the drawling tone of his voice that made her glance quickly up at him—in time to catch the speculative gleam in his eye.

He *does* think I'm up to something, she thought in dismay. It was obvious from the way he'd lingered over the words 'all alone', as if he didn't believe she *was* travelling alone. Did he suspect that she was hiding an accomplice somewhere, and that they were plotting to rob him or something?

She had better kill any suspicions quick smart or she'd be out of here on her ear before she'd learnt a thing! The way things were going, she reflected, letting a rueful smile touch her lips, it would be a race to see who learnt the most from the other first!

'I—um—saw some aspirin in the bathroom cupboard,' she murmured, sweetening her smile. 'You don't mind if I grab a couple, do you? They might help me to sleep.' She injected feminine appeal into her eyes. The sympathy vote . . . that was what she needed to cultivate.

Please, she prayed silently, if he did see anything, let him have enough compassion for me to be able to dismiss it from his mind!

She waited tensely for his answer, which came after a slight pause. 'By all means . . . use whatever is there. Call out if you need anything else. Any time of the night . . .' The silver-grey eyes held hers for a trifle longer, she thought, with a faint catch of her breath, than was strictly necessary, making her acutely aware of him as a man.

'Thank you,' she said, gulping. She forced out more. 'Thanks, Mr Corbin, for . . . everything.'

'My pleasure.' His hand briefly touched hers. 'And it's Trent.'

Her   nerve-ends   jumped   at   his   touch. 'Goodnight . . . Trent.'

She was flushing furiously as she turned and hobbled into her room. Her mind was conjuring up skin-prickling

images of him stealing into her bedroom in the dead of night, of him bending solicitously over her bed offering hot packs and slow, soothing massages and…what else?

She found she was trembling as she closed the bedroom door behind her, although not so much with apprehension at the thought of being unmasked, exposed. It was more to do with the man himself…to her emotional and physical reaction to him.

How could a man she saw as the devil incarnate—a vulture, a ruthless property shark who preyed off others less powerful and less worldly-wise than himself, who even stooped to intimidating people who stood in his way—how could a man like that make her tremble and react in this way, make her heart beat so fast, make even her bones feel weak? Her cheeks, her blood, her senses felt on fire!

She needed her head examined! What about Harry? He was the one she ought to be thinking about. She ought to be thinking about what she could be doing to help *him*.

The storm had passed over but the rain was still pattering on the roof when Trent poked his head round her door the next morning, knocking before nudging the door wider and stepping in. He was carrying a tray.

'Are you awake?'

'Y-yes, I'm awake.' She wriggled up on to one elbow, one hand hastily reaching up to brush her tangled hair from her eyes. 'I…didn't sleep all that well, I'm afraid.'

'I'm sorry to hear that. Ankle bothering you?'

She seized on the excuse. After all, it was partly true. 'A bit…but it's feeling much better now,' she said stoutly. 'The swelling's almost gone.'

'So you don't want me to call the doctor?'

'No need…thanks. It's only a sprain. It just needs rest. Are you quite sure I'm not putting you out by

staying here?' She let her gaze flutter upwards to meet his.

A silvery light flared in the grey depths. 'Stay as long as you need. You're hardly in any condition to go gallivanting on your way, even if you had a bike to ride. Ready for your breakfast?'

At a nod and a quick smile from her he handed her the tray. 'Magda hopes this meets with your approval.'

'She's very kind.' She looked down at the tray, partly to avoid that enigmatic look in his eye. What did it mean? Plenty of men had given her looks in her time, and normally she recognised them for what they were: admiring looks, warmly friendly looks, lecherous looks, even feigned indifference, tinged at times with mockery. But never...no, never a look quite like that.

'Freshly squeezed orange juice,' she murmured appreciatively. 'Scrambled eggs and bacon. Toast and tea. You're all spoiling me,' she said, smiling at the breakfast in front of her, not at him.

Even without looking up at him she sensed his withdrawal, heard it in the clipped tone of his voice, as if spoiling her was the last thing he'd had in mind. 'I'll let you get on with it, then. I have a meeting with the local council this morning. Magda will look after you. And Roland will be here, of course.'

So Trent wasn't taking his burly 'minder', as Harry had scathingly dubbed the giant, with him. He couldn't be expecting any trouble from the councillors, she concluded sourly.

'You think you'll get the support of the council?' she asked with assumed lightness as he stepped away from the bed.

He paused. 'Oh, they're fully in favour already. But there's a long way to go yet.'

'Yes, you must buy up all the properties first,' she reminded him sweetly, glancing up with an innocent air.

She saw an iron resolve harden his face. 'Oh, I'll buy them all, don't worry.' He gave a tight smile—more a grimace than a smile. 'Enjoy your breakfast, Sandra. If you want to get up later and lie on the sofa in the lounge, looking out over the sea, there's a warm fire in there.' He raised his hand in a brief salute, turned on his heel and strode out.

She was reading one of Trent's books—she'd been surprised to find he had shelves of popular biographies, thrillers and sea stories rather than the high-powered business tomes she had cynically half expected—when the blond giant Roland strolled into the lounge. Ignoring her, other than to nod briefly as he lumbered past the sofa where she was sitting with her foot up, he knelt down to add another log to the fire.

'Good morning, Roland,' she said brightly, seizing her chance to ask Trent Corbin's henchman a few cautious questions.

He grunted something unintelligible, his broad back about all she could see of him as he bent over the fire.

'Been working for Mr Corbin for long, Roland?' she asked in a pleasantly conversational tone.

'Long enough.'

A man of few words, she thought, sighing. He was wary of saying too much, obviously. Maybe he'd been warned not to. 'You find him a good boss?' she asked, adding hastily, 'He's been awfully kind to me.'

'I'd do anything for him.'

She went still. 'Anything?' she echoed, dearly tempted to ask, If he told you to vandalise someone's property, would you do that too?

'That's right.' He prodded the logs on the fire, sending sparks flying.

'Mr Corbin is fortunate to have such a loyal...um...just what *is* is that you do here, Roland?'

He shrugged. 'Whatever needs to be done, I do it. Mr Corbin knows he can rely on me. For anything.'

I'll bet, she thought, thinking of poor Harry. 'So you're a jack of all trades,' she said, injecting a teasing note into her voice. 'I take it that means you're . . . what? Caretaker? Gardener? Handyman?' She whipped in one more in the same light tone. 'Bodyguard?'

'Something like that.'

She hissed in her breath. If Trent Corbin hadn't made enemies, she thought, her lips thinning, why would he need a *bodyguard*?

'You mean . . . you sometimes have to protect him from people?' she asked, and held her breath. Could Trent Corbin possibly be involved in something shady? Even dangerous? As the thought brushed through her mind, she felt something dip inside her.

'If I have to, I will.'

'What sort of people?' she pressed, her mouth feeling dry.

He gave a shrug. 'Oh, the Press . . . cameramen . . . they're the worst. Demonstrators sometimes.'

The Press! Demonstrators! Not criminals, she thought with relief. Not that Roland would tell her!

'And . . . troublemakers?' Like her father? she wondered, her eyes narrowing. Just how far were Trent Corbin and his henchman prepared to go to drive Harry off his property?

'Sure. That's my job. I'd do anything Mr Corbin asked me to do.'

She went still. Would he be prepared to do something even worse than vandalising someone's property? Like use physical force? She wanted to ask, but didn't dare.

'You . . . must be very valuable to him, Roland,' she said evenly, aware of a prickling at her nape. 'I hope he appreciates you—and rewards you accordingly.' Which I bet he does, she thought with contempt.

'I'd do it for nothing.'

She stared at the giant's bowed back. How in the world had Trent Corbin earned such loyalty and dedication? Was working for Corbin, basking in the shadow of a powerful, influential man, enough for Roland, so that money didn't matter?

She sighed. She was becoming as cynical as Trent Corbin. *And* she was not getting very far. She certainly wasn't hearing what she had hoped to hear—some criticism of Trent Corbin, or a hint of dissatisfaction at the things Roland had seen his boss do, or seen his boss involved in, such as less than honest dealings. Roland was loyal to a fault. He would never say anything against his boss, never give anything away, she was sure of it. Not deliberately, at any rate.

'The rain seems to be easing off at last,' she commented, glancing hopefully towards the French windows. Now there was only a light sprinkling of rain outside, and the dark clouds over the ocean appeared to be lifting. 'Have you heard a weather forecast?'

The giant replaced the iron poker with a clang. 'Don't need to. Just have to look out over the sea. It'll be fine by lunchtime.'

She brightened. 'I hope you're right. I hate being shut up indoors. I like to feel the wind. Breathe the air.'

Roland grunted, this time glancing round with a raised eyebrow, looking pointedly at her bandaged ankle.

She summoned a trill of laughter. 'Yes, it would be a bit difficult at the moment, I agree. But my ankle's improving—rapidly. Once I can put some weight on it I'll try wearing shoes again—well, sneakers for a start—and then I'll be able to get about a bit more. Maybe I'll even try going for a walk.'

As she spoke the sun pierced the grey cloak of cloud outside. Her spirits lifted. With luck she might be able to hobble over to Harry's place later. If Trent went out again this afternoon.

Roland replaced the fire-screen and heaved himself to his feet. 'You plan to stay long?' he asked gruffly, eyeing her, she would have sworn, with mistrust. Had she asked too many questions? Or was it simply the protective instinct of the hired bodyguard?

'I wouldn't think so,' she said with a shrug. 'Just until I can ride my bike again. And when I *have* a bike to ride.' She flicked a tongue over her lips, and asked pointedly, 'Do you have a problem with my being here, Roland?'

He shrugged as he stepped away from the fireplace at last. 'Some women,' he growled, 'will try anything to get close to Mr Corbin.'

Her eyes sparked. 'Even try to get themselves killed?' she said tartly. 'He was the one who ran into *me*, remember!'

He paused by the sofa. 'You're the first woman he's brought here.' He almost grated the words at her. 'Don't go reading anything into it!'

She drew herself up. 'What precisely do you mean by that, Roland?'

He smirked. 'If you've got any ideas about Mr Corbin—any expectations—forget it.'

She sucked in an incredulous breath. 'You think I'm *after* him?'

'Most women are. They're either after him or his money.'

'His *money*?' She gave a snort of derision. 'I realise that to Trent Corbin and others like him money and material possessions and the acquiring of them mean everything, but I assure you, Roland, they don't to me. I have other priorities in life.'

'Oh, yes?' The close-set eyes raked over her derisively. Any charms she possessed obviously left Roland cold! 'Like what? A little fling, maybe? Or maybe even something more permanent?'

She choked back her anger, flushing at the raking scorn in the giant's gruff voice. 'Do you always insult the guests your boss invites into his home, Roland?' she asked coldly. 'Don't think I won't let him know about this!'

The pale eyes wavered. She saw him clenching his great hands into fists. 'If you knew what lengths some women are prepared to go to,' he hissed at her, 'just to get close to him, you'd understand why Mr Corbin needs people like me around.'

'I would have thought Mr Corbin was capable of fighting his own battles,' she flung back with scorn.

'Oh, he is, don't worry. But he is a busy man, and there are a lot of predatory females in the world.'

'And from what I've heard,' she retorted, flashing him a look of disdain, 'he's taken his pick of them!'

Roland's pale eyes glinted at her. 'He's a man with a normal man's impulses and appetites. But no woman will ever mean any more to Mr Corbin than *that*!' He snapped his fingers. 'Feelings never come into it, let alone anything long-term or lasting. Not since his wife and child——' He clamped his mouth shut, as if he felt it would be betraying a confidence to talk about them.

'Ah, yes.' Sandra moistened her lips. 'A terrible tragedy.' She, like most people, had heard about it, read the reports in the newspapers. 'For his wife and son to die like that . . . in a house fire. They say it took hold so quickly they had no chance. Mr Corbin, from memory,' she added, glancing enquiringly up at Roland, 'was not at home at the time. At least, not in the house . . .'

'It wasn't their home,' Roland said tersely. 'It was an old timber holiday cottage up in the mountains. Mr Corbin had gone into the forest to fetch more firewood for the wood fire while his wife and baby son were still asleep.'

'And by the time he got back,' Sandra went on, carefully keeping all expression from her voice, 'it was too late. He wasn't able to save them or the house.'

'He did all he could,' Roland lashed back. 'That came out at the inquest. Nobody could blame him.'

'No...of course not.' There had been rumours, though, she recalled. Whispers...question marks, people querying the fact that Trent Corbin alone had survived...wondering if he had been unhappy in his marriage.

The rumours had eventually died down. Or been quashed. No doubt Trent Corbin's money and influence had helped to quash them. And the result of the inquest, of course.

She realised that Roland was watching her. She met his look, her eyes steady under his. 'You need have no fear for your boss on my account, Roland.' Not the way *you* mean at least, she thought caustically. 'I assure you he is perfectly safe from my feminine wiles. I can't say I even like him much...*or* what he stands for!'

'You ungrateful bitch!' Roland spat at her. 'After what he's done for you—taking you in off the street!'

She didn't even flinch at the savage attack, facing him with fire in her eyes. 'He took me in off the street, Roland—as you so colourfully put it—because he knocked me off my bike and nearly broke my leg! He could have killed me! *And* he wrecked my brand-new bike! I'm here in his house because he was afraid I'd make trouble for him if he didn't do something for me!'

She heard a slow clapping from behind. 'So that's all you think of me.' Her head spun round, her mouth dropping open in dismay as Trent Corbin strode into the room.

'Trent, I——'

His voice rasped over hers. 'A lot of men would have dumped you at the doctor's surgery and left you there, without even offering to pay for your care *or* for your bike.' He was standing over her now, his withering expression making her shrivel inside. Was he wondering now why he had?

Her chest heaved in a ragged sigh. She had really messed things up. Curse her reckless tongue! How long, she wondered, had he been listening? The only way to get through this was to bluff it out, to fight fire with fire. A meek apology would sound false *and* give him the upper hand.

'You don't have a very high opinion of people, do you, Mr Corbin, if you think you're the only one who would have come to my aid? Is it only since you've been rich and powerful,' she demanded scathingly, 'that you've acquired this jaundiced view of life and your fellow man?'

She heard Roland's sharp intake of breath, saw Trent's eyes turn to ice above hers. Too late she remembered his wife and child. A tragedy like that would be enough to give any man a jaundiced view of life!

It was too late to back down. Besides, it was possible that he'd always been like that, even before...

She pressed on rashly, heedlessly. 'Still, I dare say it's not your fault. They say people of great wealth attract the wrong type around them. And if you're surrounded by shallow, greedy people...well...' She shrugged, feeling she'd made her point.

Glacial grey eyes held her immobile. A flick of Trent's wrist sent Roland scurrying from the room, a gloating light in his pale eyes, as if it pleased him to see them at loggerheads.

'It strikes me, Sandra, that you are the one with the low opinion of people,' Trent said harshly. 'I'm disappointed that you have such a low opinion of *me*. Is it my wealth or me personally?'

She looked up at him defiantly. 'You can't deny that your image is not a—a particularly commendable one. As portrayed by the media,' she added hastily. 'At times you come over as the devil himself, wreaking havoc and sweeping all and sundry from your path—people, properties, whatever stands in your way!' She saw a

further opening and seized it. 'You admitted yourself
that Harry—Harry Whatever-his-name-is,' she said with
a flick of her wrist, 'is standing in your way!'

To her frustration he failed to take the bait, her pre-
vious comment diverting him. 'Is that how *you* see me,
Sandra? As the devil?'

'I hardly know you,' she hedged, and stifled a sigh.
'I just know that a lot of people *do*. And they say you
don't even care. So why should you care what *I* think
of you?'

He leaned over her, his hand coming up to rest on her
shoulder. 'Oh, but I do, Sandra.' His voice was pure silk
now, his eyes glinting seductively into hers. 'I do.'

She felt her breath catch in her throat. Was that a
gleam of lust in his eyes? Or a glint of...menace? And
why wasn't she drawing back, or freezing him with her
gaze, the way she was so adept at doing with men she
didn't want to encourage? What was even worse, why
did she feel an irresistible, primitive urge to reach up
and pull him down on top of her?

Madness, sheer madness! With an almighty effort of
will, she managed to unlock her gaze from his. Masking
all expression, she fought for control, her composure in
fragments, her heart pounding, until finally she managed
to unstick her tongue. 'We were talking about your
image, not about me!' Dear God, was that high, brittle
voice her own?

He straightened slowly, his hand sliding from her
shoulder. 'I have no argument with the image I project
to the media.' The icy chill was back in his voice. 'It's
a handy image at times. It stops people from getting too
close.'

Her lips parted, his words feeling like a slap in the
face. Had she only been imagining what had happened
a moment ago? Hadn't he been trying to get
closer to *her*?

Maybe he had, she thought with a flare of cynicism, but not in the way he was talking about now. He was talking about feelings now...intimacy...all the things his henchman Roland had said he steered clear of. Trent Corbin only got close to women for one thing—for what he could get out of them, in the short term, not because he cared for them. She'd do well to remember that.

She projected her cynicism into her voice. 'From all reports, it doesn't stop women chasing after you, trying to get closer to you.' In disbelief she felt a twinge of something close to jealousy at the images that sprang into her mind.

'Oh, this is ridiculous!' she burst out, swinging her legs off the sofa. 'As if I care about your image or your women! I only care about getting my ankle better and my bike fixed so that I can get on my way again!' She stretched her arms and arched her back. 'I feel so frustrated and useless lying here!'

Let him think that was why she had reacted the way she had, why she had been firing personal questions at him.

'You need to get out of this house,' Trent agreed softly, and her heart leapt into her mouth. Was he planning to get rid of her already? Even drive her back to Sydney himself, if he had to? Or did he have something else in mind?

She held her breath, wondering what was coming.

'I'll get Magda to pack us a picnic lunch—some hot soup and sandwiches,' he drawled, 'and I'll take you for a drive around Kaoga Bay.'

'You'll...have time to do that?' she asked in surprise. With his reputation for long hours and grinding hard work—by all accounts he was a driven man who put his work above everything—a pleasant drive and a picnic lunch sounded distinctly out of character. Or was this merely the first stage of a carefully planned seduction?

Let him try! she thought disparagingly. While he's trying, I'll be probing into what makes him tick, looking for a chink in his armour. Anything that might help Harry!

'All right,' she said with an airy shrug. 'A drive around Kaoga Bay sounds fine.' She smiled up at him. 'You can show me what you find so special about this headland of yours,' she said lightly. 'And what you find so special about your neighbour Harry's property. It must be special to *him* if he's refusing to sell it to you after you've offered him the earth for it.'

Trent scowled. 'I'd prefer to steer clear of Harry's place for another day or two, certainly not show any close interest in it. He'll undoubtedly know I'm back and will be expecting me to come over and try twisting his arm again. I want him to sweat a bit longer; think I'm no longer interested.'

'Soften him up for the kill, you mean.' She hid her antagonism with an effort. 'We can still drive past, can't we, and take a look from the car?' Just a glimpse of Harry's wiry frame busily at work in his yard would be reassuring. She might be able to tell if the pressure was getting too much for him. Harry had had a mild heart attack a few months ago and the thought of him having another was always at the back of her mind. Especially now.

And there was no need to worry that Harry might recognise her—not in Trent Corbin's car!

'If you like.' Trent's mouth twisted. 'You'll wonder why Harry's making such a fuss about hanging on to his place. It's just an old cottage with a view over the sea and some land behind. Too much land for a man of his age. They say he's not as fit as he used to be.'

She caught back the stinging retort that leapt to her lips: If Harry's not as fit as he used to be, you're to blame!

Just an old cottage indeed! Oh, it's more than that, Trent Corbin, she thought bitterly. To Harry it is. It's his *home* now. And he loves it.

But would he get the chance to go on enjoying it? How long could her father hold out against a man like Trent Corbin?

CHAPTER FOUR

'YOU have *three* cars down here at Kaoga Bay?' she asked as Trent waved her to a sturdy Nissan Patrol parked outside the open double garage. His Mercedes and another smaller car were parked inside.

Trent shook his head. 'The Ford Laser is Magda's and the four-wheel drive belongs to Roland,' he said as he helped her up into the front seat. 'I'd prefer not to take the Merc. I don't want Harry to know it's me driving past, ogling his place.'

She tried to hide her disgust. How devious he was! She swung round to face him. 'But if he sees the Patrol and thinks it's Roland driving past,' she argued, 'won't that be as bad as if he thinks it's *you* spying on him? He must know that Roland works for you.'

Trent's brow lowered, as if he didn't care for the word 'spying'. She felt a stab of satisfaction that her deliberate shaft had hit home.

'Harry's used to seeing Roland driving past.' He shrugged the problem aside. 'He won't even look twice.'

She said no more, fearing that if she did he might decide to avoid Harry's place altogether.

As he backed the vehicle out of the driveway, she asked curiously, 'Is Roland married? I noticed he was wearing a wedding ring. But I haven't seen any sign of his wife.'

'You won't. She's not here.'

'She's ... left him?'

She saw Trent's brow shoot up. 'You don't like Roland much, do you?'

'Why do you say that?'

'The way you instantly thought that his wife must have left him. That...and some vibes I've picked up.'

She swallowed. Just how long *had* he been standing there listening to them earlier? 'Well, where is his wife, then?' she asked with an indifferent shrug, before he had a chance to start delving into the reasons for her antagonism.

'She's in America at the moment with her sister.'

'Oh.' If Roland could afford to send his wife for trips overseas—*and* afford a Nissan Patrol—Trent must pay him far more generously than the giant's airy dismissal of the subject of money had led her to believe.

She knew she should have left it there, but the need to know all she could about Trent Corbin and the man who worked for him urged her on. Understanding the way their minds worked could, if she was lucky, suggest some way for her to help Harry in his fight against them.

She asked carelessly, 'Roland didn't want to go overseas with his wife?' Or had Trent refused to let him go? she pondered, hiding her contempt. That would be typical. From what she'd heard about him, Trent Corbin was a cold-hearted, callous workaholic who put his needs, his projects, his ambitions ahead of the personal whims and wishes of anyone else, including, she didn't doubt, the unfortunates who worked for him.

'Sandra, just sit back and enjoy the drive,' Trent said tersely. In other words, Don't ask so many questions, she mused as she subsided, satisfied that she appeared to have hit a sore spot.

She sobered at the thought. So it was true what people said about him. He didn't care about anybody or anything. Or care a damn what anybody thought of him.

Poor Harry.

Instead of driving back across the headland the way they had come the night before, Trent pointed the vehicle the other way, following a rock-hard track towards the cliffs.

'Great view,' she commented as the track veered round to run parallel with the bald cliff-top. The sea beyond was silvery blue under the creeping rays of the late-morning sun. White tips danced on the rippled surface.

To the south the spectacular rugged coastline stretched for miles. A white froth of waves crashed over the rocks, sending spray high into the air. To the north the jutting headland, from this angle, hid most of Kaoga Bay, but she could see the steep carved cliffs and sweeping beaches further along the coast, and a sprawl of houses on the slopes behind.

'I suppose you get a better view of Kaoga Bay from round a bit further,' she said, knowing full well that 'round a bit further' was Harry's property.

'Yes, but this is as much as you'll see of it from the car,' was Trent's gravelly response. 'The track runs inland in a minute, skirting Harry's property back across the headland. The best view of the bay is from his place. And from his private cove down below. If I have anything to do with it,' he added grimly, 'it won't be private for long.'

And if Harry and *I* have anything to do with it, Sandra vowed under her breath, it will stay private!

Harry loved that cove of his, dangerous as it could be at times. He knew those cliffs like the back of his hand, and he knew the places that were safe for climbing and the rocks that were safe for fishing. But his own private cove, he insisted, was the best place in the world to go rock fishing.

He brushed off her warnings to take care, insisting that even rogue waves posed no real threat to an experienced fisherman like himself, because he always sensed when one threatened and knew how to take evasive action. She just hoped that it was true.

Trent swung the car round, following the track as it veered inland. 'This is the closest we'll get to Harry's

house,' he said, his eyes narrowing as they cruised past. 'Ugly old place, isn't it?'

'Ugly?' She swept her gaze over Harry's quaint cottage. 'How can you call it ugly? It's a charming house!'

It was too, despite Trent Corbin's jaundiced opinion of it. A charming verandaed cottage, Georgian in style, it had white walls and a grey iron roof and white paintwork round the small-paned windows. The pretty cottage garden at the front, with its central path, and the low hedge flanking the small front gate, only added to its charm.

There was no sign of Harry. He hadn't drawn the blinds or curtains, she noted, as surely he would have done if he'd gone away camping for a few days, or driven up to town.

'It's old and tired and it looks it,' Trent growled. 'The paint's peeling, the roof leaks, the veranda floor's rotting, and the front gate's nearly falling off its hinges. And the garden could do with some attention. But Harry either doesn't notice or doesn't care. As for the rooms inside,' he growled, 'they're small and low and dark. And the stairs to the attic at the back are ridiculously steep and narrow.'

He was exaggerating, finding fault for his own nefarious purposes, but she couldn't very well tell him so. To her, the place looked much the same as she remembered it from last time, the flowers in their usual rambling confusion, the tiny lawn perhaps a trifle overgrown, a few weeds starting to sprout from the honeycomb rocks bordering the lawn.

But it certainly didn't look neglected. She had to bite her tongue to keep from blurting out that Harry had been warned by his doctor to take life a bit easier and it was a pity his neighbour didn't offer him a helping hand. But of course Trent wouldn't *want* to help. He wanted to pull the place down!

'Houses can be repainted and timber floors and leaky roofs can be repaired,' she said, keeping her tone light with an effort. 'And the rooms inside…I imagine they're really cosy. And quaint.'

'The sea air hasn't helped the place,' Trent muttered as if she hadn't spoken. 'I know with my own place…you have to keep at it constantly. I'll be glad when I no longer have to bother.'

'If it's such a problem,' Sandra flashed back, seizing her chance, 'why build a resort here? Especially with winds and storms like we had last night.'

'The storms we have down here are nothing compared with the storms and cyclones they get further north during the cyclone season,' Trent said drily. 'Yet that hasn't stopped people flocking to the resorts along the Gold Coast and the Great Barrier Reef.'

Sandra didn't answer for a moment, her gaze flicking over Harry's back yard as it came into view. No sign of Harry there either. She caught a glimpse of his old car in the garage, so knew he must be around somewhere.

Most likely down in his cove, fishing.

Coming back to the subject under discussion, she said bluntly, 'The Gold Coast and the Great Barrier Reef have far more to offer. It's warm up there all year round, and the surroundings are idyllic. The resorts up there are usually built right on the beach, or on an exotic island, not stuck up on the top of a cliff.'

'There's a demand for top-class resort-style accommodation along this coast too,' Trent said, unperturbed. 'We're not necessarily targeting the international jet-set crowd or the Japanese tourists that flock to Queensland. My resort will be aimed at anyone who wants a relaxing coastal holiday in New South Wales, with fine views and a bit of luxury thrown in. Couples, retired folk, families, the lot.

'Hopefully we'll attract overseas visitors as well. People who want to fish, surf, swim, go for walks, or

simply relax in comfort. We've got a lot to offer down here too, you know.'

Sandra made no comment, instead leaning forward to remark casually, 'Your neighbour's place looks very quiet. You don't think he could be sick?' *Could* he? she wondered in swift concern. 'It must be a strain for an old man,' she added recklessly, 'being under the pressure you're subjecting him to.'

Trent's brow plunged in a frown. 'Harry's not that old. And he doesn't strike me as the type to sink under pressure. He's quite a tough old codger.'

She sucked in her breath, only just managing not to retort that Harry had had a heart attack not so long ago and wasn't as tough as he thought. 'I thought you said the place was beyond him!' she rapped back instead.

His lips narrowed. 'Well, as I said before, he either can't cope or he doesn't care enough.'

She clenched her hands into fists, tempted to lash back that it was more likely that Harry had lost heart, with the worry of the resort hanging over his head and the pressure being put on him. And the *threats*...

She sat up suddenly. 'What's that mound of earth over there?' she asked, her heart picking up a beat. She knew perfectly well what it was. It was where Harry's precious vegetable garden used to be... until someone had come in and maliciously vandalised it and dug up all his vegetables, leaving them to rot.

Trent scowled. Why the scowl? she wondered, instantly alert, instantly suspicious. Guilty conscience?

His answer was curt. 'That was Harry's vegetable patch.'

'*Was*?'

'Some kids came in and dug it up.'

She caught her breath at the blatant lie. 'Kids? What kids? How do you know that?'

He turned and looked at her, something flickering in his eyes. She could have kicked herself. Had she made him suspicious?

'How do I know about it?' he echoed drily. 'Because Harry accused me first! And don't try to pretend that you didn't have the same thought,' he added with a mocking half-smile that in the next instant he wiped from his lips. 'You honestly think I'd stoop that low to get Harry Shaw to sell to me?'

She flicked her tongue over her lips. 'A lot of people would answer yes to that,' she answered with a lift of her chin.

'Including you, Sandra?' He had slowed the vehicle to a crawl and was watching her face rather than the track ahead.

She gulped, not knowing what to say. In the second that she hesitated, he sliced in scathingly, 'Don't bother to answer that. I'm well aware what people think of me. Why should you be any different?'

'Are they *justified* in thinking that way about you?' she asked, and was unable to hide the note of anxiety in her voice, tinged with a faint yearning. But was it for herself that she wanted his reassurance or for Harry?

Trent shrugged, as if he didn't care a damn what anyone thought of him. 'In this instance,' he said caustically, nodding towards Harry's property, 'my conscience is clear. Roland swears he had nothing to do with it either, in case you're wondering.'

Was he giving her his word? But what, she asked herself disparagingly, was Trent Corbin's word worth?

'You're saying your neighbour caught the culprits in the act?' she asked, knowing full well that he hadn't.

'Hardly...or he wouldn't have accused *me*.' Trent picked up speed as they left Harry's property behind and bushland closed in on both sides. 'After getting short shrift from me,' he added, contempt hardening his voice, 'Harry reported it to the police. They were the ones who

suggested it was most likely kids. Roland told them he'd seen young kids hanging around the headland a number of times.'

'So they got the blame.' How surprising, she thought with a flare of cynicism, that the local police would rather blame youngsters than accuse Trent Corbin! Harry had said as much to her. He'd told her that the police had been most unhelpful. Trent Corbin, it was only too clear, had the whole town securely in the palm of his hand. Or, rather, in his pocket!

'Lovely neighbourhood,' she sneered, pulling a face. 'Maybe you should be doing something about the young delinquents down here rather than pandering to the pampered moneyed class!'

To her shocked surprise, Trent brought the vehicle to an abrupt halt, and twisted round to face her.

'Are you sure you don't have some personal beef against me, Sandra?' His eyes were hard with suspicion, an edge of irritation in his voice. 'If you have, spill it out now,' he invited. 'I'm all ears!'

Shocked as she was, she was sorely tempted to do just that...to tell him exactly what she thought of him and of his treatment of Harry and get it all out in the open.

But she caught herself back in time. She'd barely found out anything about him yet! Certainly nothing damaging or incriminating that she and Harry could use against him, that would discredit him and blow sky-high his plans for the headland.

If she blurted out now who she was and why she was here, she would be out of Trent Corbin's house and out of his life quicker than she could say 'Shark!' And how would she ever get another chance to be this close to him, to sneak under his guard...from the inside? She owed it to Harry to find out all she could while she had the opportunity. It would be crazy to show her hand just yet.

'You must think I'm terribly ungrateful!' she burst out, looking truly mortified as she injected feminine appeal into her uptilted blue eyes ... doing what she had always despised in other women and using her feminine wiles for all they were worth!

'It's unforgivable of me,' she went on, 'hurling abuse at you just because we don't see eye to eye on certain matters, and because I've read and heard things about you that have been—well, less than complimentary. And yet you've been more than kind to me. You're nothing like I—I imagined you must be!'

An Academy Award-winning performance, she congratulated herself as she swung her face away as if to compose herself. In actual fact, it was to avoid that keen, penetrating gaze!

'I'm forever being accused of favouring the underdog,' she confessed with a deep sigh, twisting her slender hands in her lap. It was true enough.

'So you see Harry Shaw as the underdog,' Trent said, his tone sardonic.

'Well, isn't he?' she asked unsteadily, not needing to act this time. 'From what you've told me, he's a harmless old man living alone who just wants to go fishing and grow his vegetables and be left in peace. And along *you* come—the big property developer—doing your utmost to turn his cosy little world upside down!'

She expected Trent to bite back with a lecture on progress, or a reminder of the generous compensation he was offering Harry in return and what his resort was going to mean to Kaoga Bay, or offer some other excuse to justify what he was doing, but instead he reached out his hand and touched her on the leg, just above her knee.

She nearly jumped out of her seat, the heat of his hand sending fiery prickles from her toes right up into her cheeks.

'How's your ankle standing up to the rough road?' he asked, his soothing tone, when she had been expecting a tongue-lashing, knocking her completely off-balance.

'It—it's fine.' The words came out as a pathetic croak. She was acutely aware of his hand on her leg, of the way her skin, even beneath the protective layer of denim, was tingling under his touch. Why was she reacting like this? It was crazy. She had been touched in more intimate places than this, *and* on her bare skin, by men she had liked a lot more, without feeling so much as a flutter!

She gave a trembling sigh. It's because I'm so aware of him, she decided, attempting to be clinical. Not as a man so much—a male—but as a challenge, a force to be reckoned with. This man, she brooded, is the devil in human guise. He's powerful, he's ruthless, and he's dangerous. His being tall and sexy and silver-eyed makes him doubly dangerous. An irresistible combination... to some women, she thought with disdain. There would always be women only too willing to be tempted, weakened, seduced by a sexy, good-looking villain, knowing he was dangerous, knowing he was no good for them, but unable to resist, poor fools.

Well, not me, she vowed silently. You have no power over me, Trent Corbin. I'm no more attracted to you than I am to big, beefy Roland!

At the thought of Roland, she shuddered, and stifled another shaky sigh. Who was she kidding? She hadn't reacted to *Roland* this way!

'Have you done anything about my bike yet?' she asked sharply—too sharply.

'Anxious to leave, Sandra?' Trent drawled as he withdrew his hand and pumped the accelerator, the vehicle responding with a surge forward.

She tried to ignore the seductive undertone, unsure if he was simply teasing her, mocking her for his own amusement, or issuing a veiled invitation.

'Well, have you?' she asked irritably, not prepared to play his game, whatever it was.

'Your new bike will be ready for you by the time you're fit enough to ride it.'

'My *new* bike?' she echoed. 'You mean... What about *my* bike?' she demanded. Had he decided to replace it, just like that, without even trying to get hers repaired?

'Don't worry, your new bike will be an identical model. I called in at the bike shop in Nowra this morning, which is where the nearest specialty bike shop is. Roland or I will drive down to pick it up up when it comes in later this week. They didn't have your model in stock.'

Later this week! So... she had a few more days, then. 'That's most kind of you,' she mumbled. Thanking Trent Corbin for anything was difficult. Not that there was any need to go overboard with gratitude. It wasn't as if he was doing her any special favours. He was only doing what was right and proper. *He* was the one who'd run into her and damaged her bike! And he could certainly afford to replace it.

'If you particularly need to get back to Sydney before then,' Trent said slowly, 'I could always drive you.'

She hid her dismay at the thought. Did he want her out of his life already? How could she help Harry if he bundled her back to Sydney? Not that he sounded particularly enthusiastic about driving her back. And why should he? He'd only just come down here! Presumably he had things to do, business matters to deal with.

'I wouldn't let you do that,' she said quickly. 'You have work here, and people to see. I intended resting up here for a couple of days anyway,' she assured him. 'An extra day or so is neither here nor there. I'm on leave, remember.'

'You must stay on as my guest until you're perfectly fit again.'

She smiled up at him. 'That's most kind,' she murmured.

Trent was surprised to hear himself issuing the invitation to stay on...especially as there was something about Sandra Wyatt that made him distinctly uneasy, something that told him he'd be a fool to trust her. Not that he could put his finger on what it was.

She'd been honest and open enough about her disapproval of him and his line of work. And he admired her for her honesty, irritating as he found it at times. But he had a feeling there was more to her antagonism than mere disapproval. *Was* there? And, if so, what in hell's name could it be?

Was she a friend or sister of some girl he'd had a fling with in the past and then ditched? Was she related in some way to a family he'd bought out, a family with some grievance as a result? His eyes narrowed. Could she have come here seeking some kind of vengeance?

But she hadn't sought *him* out. It was purely by chance that they'd even met. He'd knocked her off her bike, for heaven's sake! There was no way in the world she could have planned that, or known that he was coming up from behind. Hell, he could have killed her! As for bringing her back to his house, that had been his own idea, with no coaxing from her.

Still, it probably wasn't at all wise—in fact it was quite possibly insane, the most insane thing he'd done in his life—to keep her here with him at his house. A stranger. A girl he knew virtually nothing about. And, moreover, one he didn't altogether trust. But damn it, wise or not, he wanted her with him, at least for the time being. She intrigued him. Not many women in the past five years had managed to do that. And never to the extent that this girl did.

She wasn't entirely immune to him either, much as she might pretend otherwise ... and much as she might disapprove of him, and even actively dislike him. He'd felt the chemistry, the electricity between them, and it had nothing to do with their lively verbal sparring. It was a physical thing. They struck sparks off each other, and had done from the beginning. Well before she'd even known who he was.

Yes, there was chemistry between them all right, and chemistry was something that hadn't affected him since ...

Damn it, no! he thought explosively. He'd be a fool to start making comparisons. There *was* no comparison. With Celia, it hadn't been chemistry alone, and even that—the chemistry between them—had been different, gentler, not this wildness, this mad fever in his blood, this fierce yearning that made no sense. With Celia it had been love ... intimacy ... commitment. And *pain*. Agonising pain.

He groaned inwardly, silently berating himself for thinking of the two women in the same breath. He never wanted to feel that kind of pain again. He never intended to. No way would he get into a position where he could.

But a little excitement, for once. With a touch of chemistry adding spice. His eyes flicked to the girl's knee as he found himself remembering the way she had reacted to his touch.

Hell ... why not?

Trent poured her a mug of hot soup from a Thermos flask as they sat on a bench seat overlooking the broad sweep of Kaoga Bay's main beach, with the cool wind in their faces and Magda's sandwiches spread out on their laps.

There were one or two surfers in wetsuits riding the waves, and a man walking a dog, but otherwise the beach

was deserted, the long stretch of sand still dark and damp after the rain.

Sandra could see Trent Corbin's towering headland from where they were . . . and the rugged cliffs belonging to Harry's property. Her eyes swept over the tumbled rocks at the base of the cliff.

'Is that your neighbour's private cove that you were talking about?' she asked innocently, pointing to a tiny strip of beach nestled between the jutting rocks.

'Sure, that's it,' Trent said broodingly. 'You see how handy it would be for people staying at a resort up above? It's a sheltered little beach and those rocks on either side are superb for rock fishing. And access from above, though it's steep, is not difficult.'

'So that's where your neighbour...Harry...goes rock fishing,' she murmured, squinting across the water. There was no sign of Harry there now. The cove looked deserted.

'Most of the time, yes. It's his favourite spot.' Trent seemed reluctant to admit it. 'Can't see any sign of him there today, though. He must have gone fishing somewhere else. There are plenty of other spots,' he said indifferently.

She drew in a fractured breath. So uncaring! He didn't care one iota about Harry or what he must be going through. All he cared about was getting his hands on Harry's land!

She reached for her stick. ' I think I'd like to go back now,' she said, assuming a plaintive tone. 'I want to give my ankle some more heat treatment.' She limped back to the car, using the stick for support. She was walking more easily now and with less pain, but was still taking care not to put all her weight on her injured foot.

She felt Trent's hand at her elbow and her pulse skittered. 'I can manage,' she said quickly, wondering how she could be so ultra-aware of a mere touch, a polite

helping hand. Especially from *this* man. And not only aware of his touch—aware of his nearness, aware of his breath mingling with hers in the sharp sea breeze, and, above all, aware of his physical magnetism.

She was relieved when she was safely back in her seat in the four-wheel drive, with space between them.

CHAPTER FIVE

TRENT insisted that Sandra join him for dinner that evening in his dining room. Big, blond Roland was there as well, and Magda joined them at the table too, when she wasn't flitting in and out of the kitchen. Sandra was pleasantly surprised that a man as cold and unfeeling as Trent Corbin would have thought of inviting his house-keeper to sit with them.

Dinner wasn't the ordeal she had been expecting. Rather than plying her with personal questions, Trent seemed happy enough to go along with the relatively safe topics she neatly introduced herself—initially the weather and the attractions of the New South Wales south coast, then moving on to books and politics and travel and the theatre. She even found—another surprise—that they had opinions and tastes in common.

Even the reticent Roland contributed the odd word or comment on occasion, though it was obvious that he was more interested in Magda's roast beef.

It was only later, over their coffee, that Trent stepped up the heat...hoping he'd lulled her into a false sense of security? she wondered.

'So, Sandra, tell us what you do when you're not riding bikes around the countryside.' He leaned back, his coffee-cup poised at his lips.

She braced herself. 'You mean what other hobbies do I have?' she hedged.

'I mean what do you do for a living?' Trent said patiently—so patiently that she wondered if the ex-cellent Hunter Valley chardonnay at dinner had mel-lowed him.

Did a man like Trent Corbin ever mellow, ever relax, ever drop his guard? More likely he was playing some clever cat-and-mouse game, waiting for his chance to pounce!

'I...work at a sports clinic,' she answered vaguely, hoping he would be content with that and assume, like the male chauvinist she suspected he was, that she was a receptionist or an aide of some kind.

'Ah...dealing with sports injuries, I take it?' Trent drawled, his expression benign.

She nodded, shrugging, and hoped he'd leave it at that and move on to something else.

No such luck. 'You're not by any chance a doctor?' he asked slowly, his eyes probing hers.

Her chin lifted. 'Would that be so difficult to believe?' she mocked.

'Not at all. You obviously have some medical knowledge—at least of sprained ankles.' His mouth twisted slightly. 'I was thinking last night how amused you must have been when I was urging you to see a doctor. That is, if you *are* a doctor yourself?' He raised an eyebrow.

'I'm not a doctor,' she said with a wry lift of her lip. 'But I do have some medical training, or I wouldn't be working at a sports clinic.' Now, she thought hopefully, knowing she was being optimistic, will you leave it at *that*? Assume I'm just a helper, with some knowledge of first aid?

'So...what *do* you do?' he pressed. He was frowning faintly now, as if puzzled by her reticence.

She stifled a sigh. She would have to tell him. She was hopeless at lying. He'd see through her immediately. Anyway, would it really matter? There were hundreds of physiotherapists in Sydney. Surely he'd never connect her with Harry. Harry had probably never even mentioned it—or mentioned *her*, for that matter. Why should he? He and Trent were hardly convivial neighbours, exchanging friendly chit-chat.

But she still felt unsure, still couldn't bring herself to spell it out. 'Oh, massage, manipulation . . . that kind of thing,' she said offhandedly.

'You're saying you're a physiotherapist?' His eyes pierced hers. He was wondering, no doubt, why she didn't come straight out and say it.

Damn, she thought, letting her breath hiss out. Now he'll wonder why I didn't tell him in the first place, why I danced around it. If I had, he probably would have thought nothing more of it. Now it had become an issue. Now it was firmly fixed in his mind. It just might make him think of other physiotherapists he'd heard about.

Like Harry Shaw's daughter.

Damn, she cursed again. I'm simply not cut out for deception and subterfuge.

She resorted to sarcasm. 'How clever of you. That *is* what physiotherapists do. Manipulation and massage.'

She was profoundly relieved when Magda chose that moment to bustle in from the kitchen, where she had been cleaning up after dinner.

'I'll be retiring now, Mr Corbin, if you don't mind,' she said. 'I'll wash the coffee-cups in the morning.'

'You go off to bed, Magda.' Trent smiled at her, and Sandra's lips parted at the sight of it, at what it did to the hard lines of his face, to his eyes. Just as she was wishing he would smile more often it vanished, and the softening she had imagined for a second vanished with it.

She glanced up at Magda. 'Thank you for a lovely dinner, Magda.' She pushed back her chair and reached for her stick. 'I must say goodnight too.' She avoided Trent's eye. 'My foot's hurting a bit. I'd . . . better go and give it some more treatment.' Maybe, with a bit of luck, he would put her snappiness of a moment ago down to that.

'I'll come and help you,' Trent offered, rising from his chair.

Her heart gave a fluttery jump. 'I—I can do it!' She could feel her cheeks burning.

'I want to make sure it's not getting any worse,' he insisted, his hand closing round her arm. Roland, at the same time, was heaving himself out of his chair, bidding them a gruff goodnight as he lumbered out. Trent raised a hand in a brief salute as he left, though his eyes were still fixed to Sandra's flushed face.

'It's not any worse!' she croaked. Was he really concerned about her ankle? Or was it just an excuse to come into her bedroom? An excuse to get closer to her?

She felt quite weak at the thought, and had to remind herself who and what he was. He was her father's mortal enemy, for heaven's sake! He had no feelings for her father, and he would have no feelings for her either...not the kind of feelings she was looking for in a man. Trent Corbin was a man with no feelings for anyone! Even his own man Roland had said it.

Then why wasn't she protesting as he steered her from the dining room and along the passage to her room? Why was she meekly obeying him as he ordered her to lie down on her bed, and even enjoying the sensation as he sat down on the edge of the bed beside her and carefully unwrapped the bandage from round her ankle?

A tremor ran through her as he ran his fingers lightly over her faintly swollen skin.

He stopped. 'Did I hurt you?'

'No,' she whispered. She wondered if he was being genuinely solicitous, or if this was simply another step in a carefully planned campaign to seduce her.

She could feel the fever mounting inside her...tempting her to lie back and enjoy whatever he wanted to do with her.

But she mustn't...she mustn't! Tensing, like an animal sensing danger, she blurted out, 'Why are you being so kind to me? You don't even know me! You d-don't know anything about me!'

His fingers paused on her skin. As their eyes clashed, she saw surprise flicker for a brief second in the silver depths. Was it her question that had surprised him? Or the realisation that he had taken her on trust? Trent Corbin, she suspected, wouldn't take too many people on trust, women least of all.

He drew back slightly. 'Should I know something about you, Sandra?' he asked at length.

She tossed back her head, somehow meeting him in the eye without a betraying flush. 'I could be a corporate spy or something for all you know!' she heard herself retorting. Oh, hell, what was she doing? *Warning* him?

'Somehow you don't strike me as being the corporate type,' he drawled. 'A physiotherapist I can accept.'

Accept, but not altogether believe? She gave a brief laugh. 'Well, you're right about me not being the corporate type. I—I don't know anything about big business. But you didn't know that when you took me in, did you? I guess at the time,' she added musingly— anything to change the subject away from spies!—'you were more worried about the damage you might have done to me.'

'Very true,' he murmured, and idly—*or not so idly?*— brushed his fingers lightly down her bare leg. 'Mmm...your skin,' he drawled, 'is like pure silk.'

She jerked back her leg, her cheeks flaming. 'If you think, Trent Corbin,' she warned, all her nerve-ends flaring like a cat sensing danger, 'that I'm fair game, trapped here in your house with a crook ankle, you can forget it!'

Again she caught a brief spark of surprise in his eyes...or was it guilt? 'I have a feeling, Sandra,' he said, his lip taking on an ironic twist, 'that if I did try anything, with or without your approval, it wouldn't be me who came through unscathed.'

The instant the words were out he seemed to regret them, his expression closing up, his face tightening to its usual rock-hardness under her quick glance.

He rose abruptly, and stepped back away from the bed. 'I'll get you a hot towel,' he said, through almost clenched teeth.

'I—I think I'll have a hot bath instead!' she gasped, swinging her legs over the side of the bed. It seemed safer!

He nodded curtly. 'Good idea.' He turned on his heel. 'I'll leave you to it. Sleep well, Sandra.'

This time there was no mocking 'pleasant dreams' as he strode from the room, vanishing without a backward glance.

It was Magda who brought in her breakfast tray the next morning.

'Oh, Magda, this is sweet of you but there's really no need any more.' Sandra was already dressed and about to leave the room. 'I can have my breakfast with everyone else.'

'They've already had theirs,' Magda said, putting the tray down on the bed. 'Mr Corbin's working in his office and Roland is out in the garden. You put your feet up and enjoy it.'

'Well, tomorrow, if I'm still here,' Sandra said firmly, 'I'll get up a bit earlier and join you all.'

'You're thinking of leaving...already?' Magda paused on her way out. 'But your ankle...' She glanced down at Sandra's bandaged foot. 'You need to give it time, lass. Anyway, you can't leave yet. Your new bike's not ready.'

Sandra gave her a smile, her heart warmed by the woman's friendliness. 'Well, we'll see.' Trent might kick her out before then. He certainly would if he found out who she was.

*   *   *

As she passed by Trent's office later she heard voices. She realised he was playing back his answering machine. On an impulse she knocked on the door and poked her head into the room.

'Good morning.' She glanced past him to the papers scattered over his desk and poking from his fax machine. What was he working on? The plans for his new resort? Another take-over bid or buy-out? Some other disrupting deal? Disrupting, that was, not to him but to somebody else!

'Ah, Sandra.' He waved her in, making no attempt to hide any of the papers. 'Excuse the mess. My secretary's holding the fort back in town and she keeps sending me faxes and phone messages,' he said ruefully. 'I'm finding it hard to keep up.'

Her heart gave a tiny flutter. He'd given her just the opening she'd been hoping for! 'Is there anything I can do... to earn my bed and board?' she offered, adding, 'I'm not the type to loll around reading books all day. I like to be useful.'

He looked at her for a disconcertingly long moment. 'Can you use a fax machine?' he asked at length.

'Sure. And a word processor.' All the physios at the clinic had their own PCs and shared a fax machine. 'Just tell me what you want done and I'll do it.' She was surprised to find him even considering her offer. Wasn't he afraid she might see something she shouldn't?

'You could send some faxes for me, if you wouldn't mind.' As he spoke his eyelids flickered under her gaze, as if his request had surprised him as much as it had her. 'I've already written them out, ready to send. It'll save me a few minutes of my time.

'And you could answer the phone if it rings,' he added, scrawling a few notes on a pad. 'If any of these people call, this is what I want you to tell them. If they want to speak to me personally, I'm not here, understand? If

it's anyone else, take a message and their number and tell them I'll get back to them.'

He didn't seem concerned about who might call. Didn't he have anything to hide after all?

He handed her the notepad and she ran her eyes down the list of messages. One name leapt out at her. Tiffany Edwards.

She knew the name. And the face. Most people would. Tiffany was a high-profile figure—public relations officer for Sydney's top department store. She often appeared on TV or in the papers doing a promotion or attending some high-society function, usually on the arm of an equally high-powered businessman. In recent months she had been photographed with Trent Corbin at the theatre and various places around town.

The message Trent wanted her to give Tiffany was brief. 'Sorry, unable to come back to Sydney at present. Give my ticket to another admirer. Enjoy Pavarotti.'

She blinked. Was his work down here more important to him than a Pavarotti concert? If he really wanted to go, really wanted to see Tiffany, surely he could slip up for the evening and come back again the next day? It was only a couple of hours away by car.

She eyed him speculatively. And why didn't he want to tell her himself? Could he be cooling off her? Backing off, perhaps, because he didn't want to get any more involved? She compressed her lips. It seemed to confirm what everyone said—that with Trent Corbin it was always work first, women second; he never risked getting emotionally involved.

'Something wrong, Sandra?'

She blinked, and swallowed. 'You're saying no to a *Pavarotti* concert?' she asked, careful not to bring Tiffany Edwards' name into it.

'On this occasion, yes. Why...? Do you expect me to go haring off to Sydney, leaving my house guest?' A mocking eyebrow shot up.

Leaving her to her own devices, did he mean?

'You don't have to stay here and entertain me,' she said loftily. 'I can look after myself. You have plenty of good books here. And there's TV...'

'I don't *want* to go.' The words were firm and final. 'The letters I want you to fax are here by the machine. Yell out if you need any help. I'll be at my desk in the other room.'

He vanished through a doorway into what she assumed was his inner office, not bothering to shut the door behind him.

She picked up the first handwritten fax and placed it in the machine. It concerned a directors' meeting. The next fax discussed a building project. Not a high-powered office building or housing estate but a rehabilitation centre! There was a communication to the council, a fax confirming a contract, another accepting an invitation to a business luncheon. Nothing the least bit incriminating or shady, as far as she could tell.

As she was waiting for the faxes to go through, she glanced idly down at the other papers scattered on the desk.

Her eyes dilated. They were all requests for donations. An art gallery, an animal shelter, a marina down the coast, a recreation centre, an artists' group, a couple of obscure societies, even one or two overseas organisations. All had a red line slashed across them, with the word 'no' scrawled on top.

Typical, she thought indignantly. He's refused them all! Trent Corbin is only interested in *making* money, not giving it away!

Tight-lipped, she ripped out the fax that had just gone through and whipped in another—just as the phone rang. It was Tiffany Edwards, demanding to speak to Trent.

'I'm afraid Mr Corbin isn't available at present,' she said in her politest tone. 'But he has——'

'Who are you?' Tiffany cut in sharply.

'Sandra Wyatt. I'm doing some secretarial work for Mr Corbin.'

'Oh, yeah? I'll bet. Put him on.'

'I'm sorry, but he's not here at the moment. He left a message for you.' She swallowed and relayed Trent's message about the Pavarotti concert.

A stream of colourful invective shrilled in her ear. When it finally died down Sandra asked tentatively, 'Do you want me to give him any message in reply?'

'Get him to ring me the second he comes in!' The phone crashed down.

By the time Trent emerged from his inner office for their lunch-break she had finished sending all the faxes and taken a number of calls. She handed him a list of the ones that had come in.

'You've been a great help,' he said, smiling in the same way he had smiled at Magda last night. Her heart rolled slowly over. No wonder Tiffany was smitten, she thought, trying with difficulty to harden her heart against him.

'Tiffany Edwards wants you to ring her,' she told him, keeping all expression from her face—and her voice.

'Then Tiffany's going to be waiting,' he said, his smile vanishing. 'If she rings again tell her I'm not going to be available for some time.' He switched on the answering machine before ushering her out.

She bit her lip. 'Don't you think you should tell her that yourself?' she ventured.

He scowled. 'I have told her. Just do it!'

After their light lunch of quiche and salad, as she was typing a letter Trent had asked her to type, Tiffany called again.

'Is he back yet?'

'I'm sorry. He's...still not available. He's going to be tied up, he says, for some time.'

'So...' Tiffany's voice took on a malicious edge '...he's found someone else, has he? *You*, I suppose? Well, good

luck to you! Enjoy it while it lasts!' The phone slammed in her ear.

Sandra drew in a tremulous breath. You don't need to warn me, Tiffany, she thought with a sigh. I know the kind of man he is.

She finished typing the letter, and the envelope to go with it, and took them in to Trent, mentioning Tiffany's call at the same time. 'Is there anything else you'd like me to do?' she asked coolly, noting that he hadn't rushed to hide anything from her as she'd come in.

'You've been a life-saver,' he said. 'Just one more thing.' He bent down to scribble something on a piece of paper. 'Ring this florist, will you, and send some flowers to Tiffany? I've written down her address too. Anything but red roses.'

Red roses for love . . . No, he wouldn't want red roses. 'Any message?' she asked impassively.

'Hmm.' He pursed his lips, and wrote something else. 'This should do it.' He handed it to her and turned back to his desk.

She glanced down at what he'd written. 'All things have to come to an end. Thank you for the good times we had. Trent.'

Simple as that, she thought. Curt and to the point. Tiffany is out. Who's next? *Me?*

Drawing in a deep breath, she moved back to the phone, rang the florist, and then reported back to Trent.

'Thanks, Sandra.' He made no other comment. Tiffany was history. 'Why don't you take a break now?' He smiled, and again her senses leapt at the sight of it. This is *Trent Corbin*, you fool, she berated herself. But her brain and her senses seemed to have no connection any more. 'Go and give your foot a rest,' he suggested.

'I have been resting it. Um . . . do you mind if I go out for a walk?' she asked airily, seizing her chance. 'I could do with some fresh air. I won't go far,' she was quick to add. 'Needless to say.'

'I'll come with you.' Trent pushed back his chair.

'No need to do that!' she said at once, hiding her dismay. How could she go and see Harry if Trent was with her? 'Go on with what you're doing. I won't come to any grief.'

'Having caused your injury in the first place,' Trent insisted drily as he rose from his desk, 'I consider myself responsible for your safety and well-being while you're in my care. Naturally I will come with you.' He moved over to switch on the answering machine. 'There! Shall we go?'

She cursed silently. 'You're being far too kind,' she said without encouragement, adding lightly, 'I'm sure you have more important things to do with your time than traipsing around the cliffs with a lame duck.' She was careful not to look directly at him, not wanting him to think that she was issuing a challenge, or, heaven forbid, being provocative.

Trent glanced down at her, but all he said—silkily— was, 'Nevertheless I shall come with you. We can both work up an appetite for dinner.'

She backed out with a frustrated sigh. What if Harry happened to see her out on the headland with Trent and called out to her? Her cover would be blown!

'I'll go and get my waterproof jacket—it'll be cold out on the cliffs,' she mumbled, knowing it had a hood that she could pull up over her head.

When she met up with him again, she made one last attempt to stop him coming with her, drawing in a sharp breath as if she had just remembered something.

'What if that neighbour of yours...Harry...sees you? I was planning to go for a walk along the cliff path I saw yesterday from the car. If your neighbour gets the idea you're out there nosing around his property...that you're still interested in it...' She paused meaningfully and shrugged. 'I thought you wanted him to sweat.'

Trent looked down at her, his eyes speculative under his heavy brows. She had the uneasy sensation that he was reading her mind. Or trying his hardest to.

'You would dearly love to see me fail in this resort project, wouldn't you, Sandra?' he said at length, his tone sardonic.

Her eyes gleamed. Would she ever! Why hide it? 'I did tell you I tend to take the side of the underdog.' She smiled sweetly as she said it, but there was a steely purpose and a hint of indignation behind her smile. 'I feel sorry for people who don't have the power or the influence—or the wealth—to fight for themselves. Or a name,' she added for good measure, 'that carries any weight. Believe it nor not, there are plenty of other people who think the way I do.'

Not that you'd care, she thought as she faced him steadily, defiance in the brave tilt of her chin.

His eyes glittered under her gaze; that was his only reaction. Instead of subjecting her to a scornful backlash, or attempting to defend himself, he muttered with an indifferent shrug, 'Harry won't know it's me. Not if I wear Roland's parka.' He ripped off his jacket and, with an almost boyishly wicked grin, exchanged it for Roland's heavy parka, dragging its hood up over his head.

Diabolical, she fumed in silence. The man is *diabolical*. She just hoped that her father—if he happened to catch sight of them—would see through Trent's cunning little subterfuge—without recognising her at the same time. And, above all, she hoped that he would see through the scheming devil's calculating waiting game...see it for what it was—yet another low-down tactic to get Trent Corbin what he wanted!

CHAPTER SIX

'CAREFUL!' Trent warned as Sandra stepped off the cliff
path to peer down over the edge of the windswept cliff,
pretending to be watching the sea bubbling and swirling
around the rocks way down below, but in reality trying
to catch a glimpse of Harry's secluded cove further
round.

But from here the jut of the cliffs kept it safely hidden
from prying eyes.

'Keep away from the edge!' Trent bit out sharply, his
hand flashing out as she strained forward. Clamping his
hand over her wrist, he jerked her back, shocking her
further by dragging her hard up against his body instead
of letting her go. Her hood slipped back from her head,
letting her golden hair stream free in the wind.

At once she felt his fingers clawing up through the
loosened strands, his hand balling into a fist round the
hair at her nape. Tears sprang to her eyes as he pulled
her head back, forcing her to face him.

'What are you trying to do...kill yourself?' His breath
was hot on her face.

With a gasp she blinked the tears away, her eyes
snapping wide. The second her startled gaze met his his
head swooped down and his mouth captured hers, the
fingers twisted in her hair giving her no chance to pull
back, no hope of escaping the hungry pressure of his
lips.

But escape, for a few dazed seconds, was the last thing
on her mind as her stunned senses absorbed the hot,
spicy taste of his mouth and a honeyed weakness in-
vaded her limbs. When his tongue softly probed the

moistness inside her mouth she felt as if her breath would choke in her throat, a delicious melting heat fountaining up from deep inside her and spreading like wildfire through her quivering body.

A sudden sharp gust of wind buffeted them, knocking her back to the reality of where she was... and with whom. With an angry whimper of protest against the seductive motion of his lips, she wrenched her mouth away from his, wincing as she felt another sharp tug at her hair, tears again filling her eyes. At once he relaxed his grip, rubbing his hand soothingly over her smarting nape, leaving her blinking in relief. And hopping mad.

'What do you think you're doing?' she snarled at him, pulling back away from him to prevent him from feeling the way her heart was pounding against his, even through the cushioning layers of waterproof, and using raw fury to cover her recklessly foolish moment of weakness.

'Kissing you,' he said calmly, his eyes glittering with mockery. 'What did you think I was doing?' He was still holding her and he was still far too close, his warm breath fanning her face. Even as he spoke his fingers were digging into her arms through the sleeves of her jacket, as if he was about to drag her up against him again.

Afraid that she would be lost if he did, she forced her body to stiffen, her chin to lift. 'Well, you can stop kissing me right here and now,' she said imperiously, if a trifle unsteadily, 'and let go of me!'

She wouldn't demean herself by struggling. In a physical struggle she knew she would be no match for him. It would be stupid to betray any further sign of weakness, or lack of control. Better to use her other strengths to defeat him—her authority, her spirit, her pride.

'It was only a kiss, Sandra.' His lips curled in a taunting half-smile.

Only a kiss! She blocked from her mind the effect his kiss had had on her, focusing instead on his intent. Since

when, her eyes demanded scathingly, are men like you, Trent Corbin, ever content to stop at a kiss? A kiss, to a man like you, is only the beginning, the first step to a full-scale seduction!

She stifled a treacherously shivery thrill at the thought and summoned a look of raging scorn. 'Just don't get the idea you can repeat it any time you like! And don't go thinking you can try anything else, either!' she added for good measure.

'I'd *like* to do more than just kiss you,' Trent drawled, sliding his tongue over his lips in sensual invitation. 'A lot more.'

Her mouth went dry. 'I'll just bet you would!' she bit back viciously, hating the unsteadiness she heard beneath her valiant show of indignation.

'Afraid, Sandra?' he taunted, as if he had heard it too.

She tilted her chin a notch higher. 'Of you?' she said in a tone of withering scorn.

'I was thinking rather of your own responses.' His lips curved in sardonic satisfaction.

She flushed. 'If it seemed like a response to you, you forced it!' she snapped, with a sharp toss of her head. 'Sorry to disappoint you, but not all women are ready to fall into your arms at a snap of your fingers, Trent Corbin. Or into your bed,' she warned savagely.

'I only kissed you, Sandra.' Amusement glittered in his eyes. Now he was laughing at her! 'No need to look so outraged.'

'I'm not outraged, I'm…disgusted. I—I hated it,' she lied.

'I'd love to see the way you respond when you *enjoy* a kiss,' he said ungallantly, the corner of his mouth lifting further. 'Shall we give it another try?' he challenged, with a wicked leer.

Her eyes widened in alarm as his hands increased their pressure on her arms and she felt him urging her—oh, so slowly—inexorably closer.

'No, you don't!' She threw back her head, twisting away from him as his face swayed seductively over hers. 'You can't help yourself, can you?' she sneered, her voice shrill with scorn, and brittle at the edges with apprehension—and...excitement? 'I would have thought you'd have learned your lesson!' she lashed out in desperation.

He froze. 'Meaning?' He frowned into her face.

She hesitated, but only for a second, then persisted recklessly, 'Meaning you've been burnt at least once already by your hormones running out of control!'

The hands on her arms turned to iron clamps, his fingers biting into her flesh through her waterproof jacket. She gulped under his fury as his frown turned savage.

'My hormones never run out of control,' he rasped. '*I* never lose control.'

'I—I see,' she said, trying to rally her courage. She'd gone this far. She couldn't back off now. 'But you d-don't face the consequences of your *controlled* hormones either, do you?' she accused rashly.

'What the hell are you talking about?' His voice was dangerously low now, frightening her even more than the fierce vibrations she felt pulsing from him.

Somehow she managed to face him without outwardly flinching. 'I'm talking about that woman who slapped a paternity suit on you a few months ago!'

A brief, demonic flame glowed in his eyes. 'Oh? And what precisely do you know about that?' he ground out.

She eyed him warily. 'Only what I—I've read in the papers. You're a high-profile person,' she reminded him tartly. 'You can't expect the Press to ignore a thing like——'

'She retracted—publicly,' he sliced in. 'Did you read *that*?' he asked caustically. 'Well, did you?' He gave her an impatient shake.

She flicked her tongue over her lips. 'You're saying—you never even slept with her?'

'I'm saying she had no case against me.' His tone was coldly contemptuous. 'And she knew it.'

Sandra gave him a long, hard look. 'I suppose you paid her off or . . . or threatened her,' she breathed, condemnation deepening the blue of her eyes—and covering a flicker of pain. 'If you slept with her, how could you know that she didn't . . . that she wasn't . . . ?' She trailed off with a careless jerk of her shoulder.

'You think if I slept with a woman I'd be fool enough not to take precautions?'

'Maybe your precautions weren't good enough!' she snapped back.

'If you prefer to cast me as the villain, Sandra, feel free.' He sounded bored now, indifferent.

'You don't need me to cast you in the role of villain!' she flung back with biting scorn. 'You've made the role into an art form! Is it any wonder people believe the worst of you? You've always made it clear that you don't care about people, or about their feelings, or about what you do to their lives!'

Before he could slip in a retort she rushed on breathlessly, deciding that she might as well spill it all out, now that she'd gone this far.

'You've made no secret of the fact that you only care about your ruthless quest for more and more property. And more and more *money*. I bet you used your money and your influence to shut the poor woman up.

'Who's going to believe a woman with no name or money or influence to back her up, when she's up against a man like you? I bet you made sure you pointed that out to her, too, before you bought her off! And I bet

you bought your way out of having to take a blood test—
or whatever it is one has to do in these sordid cases!'

His eyes seared over her face for a frighteningly
dangerous moment, and she quivered under his black
gaze. For a second she felt a flare of real fear. He was
still holding on to her... and they were still only a step
or two from the sheer edge of the cliff!

She met his hard gaze, for a fleeting second showing
her fear, her panic.

'Don't think it's not tempting,' Trent muttered, and
she gasped as he almost lifted her off her feet—but it
was to drag her further away from the edge, not closer
to it.

She ran her tongue over bone-dry lips, her gaze fluttering under his.

'For pity's sake, Sandra, you didn't honestly believe——' Trent took one look at her face and pulled
her into the curve of his shoulder. 'I may be guilty of a
lot of things,' he growled, 'but pushing females over cliffs
isn't one of them. Even under the severest provocation!'

She buried her face in his shoulder, wondering if he
could say the same about people who stood in his way—
people like Harry. Yet even as the doubt flashed through
her brain she was wondering how his shoulder could feel
so warm and safe. How could she feel *safe* with him,
after what she had just been thinking?

'My God, you did believe it!' Trent, feeling the tremor
that shook through her, began to move the warm palm
of his hand over her back, rotating it gently. 'I'm sorry
that you see me as such an ogre, Sandra,' he said without
expression. 'I may have faults—possibly more than
most—but I don't stoop to violence, I promise you!'

She shivered, this time under the sensuous motion of
his hand on her spine. Foolishly, perhaps, she believed
him. Trent Corbin might be a cold-hearted, unfeeling
devil in many ways, but he wasn't a violent man, she
was sure of it.

But he didn't know yet that she was Harry Shaw's daughter. It might be a different matter when he found out!

She groaned, only realising that she had done so aloud when Trent drew back his head and looked down at her, his eyes piercingly silver, piercingly sharp, seeming to see right into her soul.

She let her gaze flutter away, her eyelashes sweeping down over her flushed cheeks.

'Hell, I really did frighten you,' he muttered, a faintly baffled note in his voice now.

Her eyes leapt back to his. If he demanded to know *why* she should be frightened of him... She sucked in her breath, casting around wildly for a diversion. Anything...

Only one thing came to mind. 'D-don't be silly. I...I was thinking of something else entirely,' she lied. 'I was thinking of that poor woman...wondering how she must be feeling...with a child whose father won't acknowledge it!'

Trent stiffened, his eyes turning to ice, his face hardening. She felt him withdraw from her, felt his hand slide from her back, his other hand slackening its grip on her arm. 'So you choose to believe her, not me. So be it.'

His tone was coldly remote. More indifferent than angry, she thought in swift indignation. As if he didn't care whether she or anyone else believed him or not. As if the consequences of his actions were of no concern to him.

That was what incensed her, and prompted her to lash back at him impetuously—the fact that he didn't even seem to care...about the woman, or her child, or indeed anything at all...Harry included. Suddenly she wanted to pierce that cold indifference, to hurt him if she could, to make him feel *something*.

'Where there's smoke there's usually fire, so they say!' she bit back, referring to the paternity suit. But the in-

stant the words were out she realised they could be taken
another way, and clapped a hand to her mouth, her face
blanching in dismay at her unwitting cruelty.

'So... you know about that too.' Trent's voice was an
icy rasp, his silver eyes—devil's eyes—darkening to cold
steel.

She gulped. 'Trent, I—I didn't——'

'Mean it?' he sliced over her. 'Maybe not. But you
obviously know about it. Just how much *do* you know?'

Her parted lips trembled under the withering contempt in his voice. She lifted her chin, summoning her
only defence. 'J-just what I've read in the papers...seen
on TV. Trent, I'm sorry...'

'Spare me your pity!' He speared a look down at her,
his eyes narrowing as they caught the wavering doubt in
hers. 'Or am I being too hopeful?' he sneered, his scorn
biting into her. 'No doubt——' a mirthless smile touched
his lips '—you've come to the same conclusion as
everyone else—that I deserve to be strung up, not pitied!'

Her teeth tugged at her lip, for a brief second holding
back the doubts and uncertainties that she couldn't deny.
It was her anger over his treatment of Harry that finally
loosened her tongue.

'What do you expect people to think,' she burst out,
'when you refused to utter a single word in your own
defence? You didn't even look as if you *cared*. I—I saw
you on television at the funeral of your—your wife and
child. You showed no distress, no pain, no
anger...nothing! It was the same at the inquest. Not a
word of regret or remorse passed your lips afterwards.
It—it was chilling.'

She'd thought at the time how unnatural it was for a
husband to show such a lack of emotion after such a
shocking tragedy. A tragedy, moreover, that *he* had
caused—unwittingly or otherwise.

He was the one who had set alight the log fire which
had sparked off the inferno in his family's small holiday

cottage, the heavy smoke and fumes suffocating his sleeping wife and child in their beds even before the deadly flames reached them...while he was safely outside in the forest, reportedly fetching more logs for the fire.

'I don't bare my soul in public,' Trent grated with contempt. 'Not even to stop rumours.'

She slanted a sceptical look up at him. 'If a person feels deep pain and grief, it's not so easy to hide it.'

'But it's easy enough to fake it,' he bit back.

She let that sink in for a moment, and had to concede that that was true. Surely a guilty husband would have *shown* some distress...some remorse...and looked for sympathy?

'Well, you were exonerated, so you needn't worry, need you?' she said, hoping for Harry's sake—only for Harry's?—that Trent Corbin *wasn't* the cold-hearted monster that people believed him to be...that he'd never made any effort to publicly deny.

Fortunately for Trent Corbin, the coroner hadn't shared the public's harsh opinion, showing evidence at the inquest that a protective screen had been found in front of the fireplace. A stray spark from the fire was believed to have spat out over the top of the screen and ignited the floor rug and curtains, causing the timber cottage to explode into a ball of flame within minutes.

The coroner had also revealed how holiday-makers from nearby cottages had rushed to the scene, but by then it had been too late. They had arrived just in time to restrain Trent Corbin from diving into the inferno in a vain attempt to save his family.

There had been rumours even about that, she recalled, whispers that Trent Corbin had purposely arrived too late at the scene, that he had tired of his marriage and had wanted the freedom to pursue his old bachelor existence—which, it had been maliciously pointed out, he had kept up ever since the tragedy, not choosing to marry a second time. If the man was genuinely grieving,

people had whispered in disgust, why hadn't he shown some sign of it? If he was truly innocent, why hadn't he spoken up for himself at the inquest?

They had shaken their heads when the coroner had brought in a finding of death by misadventure.

The doubts and questions had lingered ever since. And Trent Corbin's callous disregard for people, his ruthless business practices, and the sleekly beautiful women he was photographed with from time to time—mostly hard-nosed, sophisticated businesswomen who looked as cold-hearted and ambitious as himself—women like Tiffany Edwards—had kept the rumours from dying a natural death.

Using her stick, Sandra swung on her heel and moved away from him, remembering to pull her hood back over her head as she stomped off along the path.

'Look, why don't you go back?' she muttered over her shoulder. 'You have your work to do. I'll wander back later, taking my time. I'll be careful, I promise.'

'As I told you before, you're my responsibility.' He caught up with her, irritation tightening his mouth. Was it because they were nearing Harry's place? she wondered. 'And you've shown that you need someone to keep you away from . . . danger.'

And to keep an eye on her? She stifled a sigh. 'Come with me by all means,' she said, giving an indifferent shrug as she limped on. 'Don't blame me if your neighbour recognises you. Up close nobody could mistake you for Roland,' she pointed out maliciously. 'You're tall, but you're not exactly a giant.'

'Too bad if Harry sees me.' Trent shrugged off his irritation. 'It might not be such a bad thing. Having him see me out taking a walk but not bothering to come and visit him . . .' His lip curved. 'Yes, that should convince him I've really lost interest.'

'I'm sure he wouldn't be that stupid!' she snapped, frustrated that he was insisting on coming with her. What

if Harry recognised *her* while she had Trent with her? She huddled deeper into the concealing hood, cursing inwardly—and cursing Trent Corbin most of all!

'You're always so cool, so sure of yourself, aren't you?' she erupted, her uncertainty and frustration fraying her nerves to bursting point. 'Always so sure you're going to come out on top!'

'In your case, Sandra, I'd be content with any position,' Trent drawled, the taunting smile on his lips— almost a leer!—making his meaning plain.

She couldn't speak for a second, heat flashing along her cheekbones. 'I was talking about your fight for Harry's land!' she snapped back, finally managing to find her voice, her flush deepening as she heard a betraying quiver under the shrillness.

The mocking smile widened—and then was gone, his tone sober as he assured her, 'It's a fair fight, Sandra…whatever you might think. Harry will be getting far more than his place is worth. *And* a better place to live. I'll make sure of that. Tomorrow I'm going down the coast to look at a house that's coming up for sale. If it's as good as I think it is, I'll present it to Harry on a platter.'

Her heart gave a tiny flutter. While he was away from the house tomorrow…

'Will Roland be going with you?' she asked carelessly. 'I don't fancy being left with him, that's all,' she added hastily as she felt his eyes burning into her averted profile.

After a discomfiting pause, he answered. 'He is, as it happens. I'll need him to drive. There are some plans I want to examine on the way down.'

She hid her jubilation with an effort. Both Trent and Roland gone for the day! What a chance to go and see Harry, without having to look over her shoulder every second!

But her jubilation was short-lived. 'You can come with me,' Trent said smoothly. 'It will be a pleasant drive for you.'

She inhaled long and deeply, casting around wildly for an excuse. 'Oh, no, I couldn't!' she protested, grabbing at the only excuse she could think of. 'You'll be wanting to concentrate on your plans. And you'll be seeing estate agents and—and signing documents and things. It's your business, Trent, nothing to do with me.'

She realised that they were coming dangerously close to the front of Harry's quaint cottage. There was no sign of Harry, she noted with relief.

'Besides,' she added, plucking another excuse out of the air, 'I'd rather be exercising my foot than sitting cramped up in a car all day. It's important that I keep mobile, get some strength back into it.'

'As you wish.'

She swallowed. He had given in more quickly than she'd expected. Was he secretly glad of the chance to get away from her for a few hours? She hadn't been exactly friendly. Far from it—she'd attacked him on all fronts.

Maybe that had been a mistake. Maybe from now on she should be a bit nicer to him . . . less judgemental. So that he would be less on his guard against her, and, as a result, be more likely to let something slip, even inadvertently allude to some dubious business deal he was involved in. Something that she could use against him to help Harry in his fight to keep his home. A slim hope, she realised, but one never knew.

She turned to face him. 'I think I've had enough exercise for today,' she asserted, lifting her foot off the ground to give her ankle a rest. 'Do you mind if we go back now? I'd like to get back and take a soothing bath. If that's all right with you?'

She wiped out all trace of her antagonism—and every other negative feeling she had for him—as she looked up into his face, hoping that their walk in the bracing

wind would have added a sparkle to the clean blue of her eyes.

But it was she who felt the jolt as their eyes met. He'd felt *something* ... she sensed it immediately, instinctively. But whatever it was *she* was the one who went weak at the knees, so that she almost lost her balance for a second. She felt a burning in her cheeks as he caught her arm to steady her.

'Sorry; I guess I'm not used to standing on one leg!' she gasped, feeling flustered and confused. 'I—I was just trying to rest my ankle for a bit.'

His arm slid round her waist, his grip firm and steady as a rock. 'Lean on me,' he invited, his voice a deep rumble that seemed to go right through her and roll around inside. 'Hold your foot up off the ground and let me take your weight on the way back. Just use your good leg to hop along.'

'Thank you,' she breathed, giving in with a good grace and smiling sweetly up at him. Yes, this was the best way to deal with Trent Corbin, she decided smugly, trying hard to ignore the fact that she *liked* being so close to him, *liked* having his support, even liked the feel of his muscular arm clasping her close to his side, so securely that she could feel his hard, sinewy muscles moving against her body with every step.

Being feminine and helpless, appealing to the man's chivalry, she told herself, was likely to get her a lot further than fighting with him and challenging him the whole time. A *whole* lot further!

CHAPTER SEVEN

'DON'T linger too long in your bath, Sandra,' Trent said as they parted in the passage. 'I'm taking you out to dinner.'

Her eyes flew to his. 'You are?'

'I have to drop some documents off and have them signed. It means driving to a town about fifteen minutes from here. There's a particularly fine restaurant there. Can you be ready in an hour?'

She chewed on her lip. 'I—I don't have a dress. Or any decent shoes. And with this bandage on my foot...'

'No need to dress up. You're not in the city now. Trousers will be fine. And flat-heeled shoes. I'm sure you'll find some trousers and a dressy blouse in my sister's wardrobe, if you don't have anything suitable. You'll come?'

She nodded. 'Sounds good. And it will give Magda a break,' she said, not wanting him to think she was jumping at the invitation solely because of him.

He tilted his head at her. 'No wonder Magda likes you,' he muttered as he swung away. She thought she saw a spark of surprise in his eyes as they flicked away from hers.

'Well, you have scrubbed up well.'

'Thank you.' She smiled up at him. It had felt good to dress up a bit, even if it was in his sister's cast-aside clothes. Her reflection in the mirror had told her that the cream embroidered blouse and wide-legged burgundy trousers she'd found in the wardrobe, and her own gold-buckled belt, flattered her slender figure and fair

colouring. The bandage could barely be seen. Her hair, freshly washed and dried with a hair-dryer provided by Magda, gleamed with gold highlights.

How many other women, she wondered idly as Trent led her out to his car, had made use of his sister's clothes? And then she recalled Roland telling her that she was the first woman Trent had invited into this cliff-top home. Which meant that not even Tiffany had come down here.

Of course, her own case was rather different. Trent had almost been *forced* to bring her home—a helpless stranger he'd knocked off her bike!

The town Trent drove to was inland from the coast, a charming little town with a row of neat shops and office buildings in an immaculately kept main street. He had no trouble finding a parking spot close to the office he had to visit. He invited her to go in with him. She nodded, surprised that he hadn't decided to leave her sitting in the car.

It was a legal office, she noted. There were a few people still inside, obviously working late. The lawyer Trent had come to see called them into his office and ran his eyes over the documents Trent handed him.

'They look fine,' he said as he signed them. 'You're a tough negotiator, Trent Corbin, but I have to say this about you. You always abide by what you agree to. And your dealings are always fair. Good to do business with you.'

They shook hands, and Trent led her out. Well, she thought, hiding a grimace, so his dealings are always fair, are they? That was not altogether what she had wanted to hear!

The restaurant he took her to was an old converted house, very cosy inside with a warm fire glowing in the grate. The proprietor seemed pleased to see Trent, greeting him by name.

'First time we've seen you here with a young lady, Mr Corbin,' the man remarked teasingly, giving Sandra a smile.

Trent didn't smile back. 'Miss Wyatt has been doing some secretarial work for me,' he said curtly, not mentioning her sprained ankle or the fact that she was staying with him as a result of it. Maybe he was trying to protect his reputation—or *hers*? Or was it simply that he didn't want to give the man any false ideas?

Most of the tables in the softly lit restaurant were already occupied. Sandra felt curious eyes following them as the proprietor led them to a small table against the wall.

Trent didn't even glance round to see if he knew anyone there. His eyes were solely for her as they sat down opposite each other.

'Like a drink before dinner?' he asked. 'A glass of champagne?' His eyes lingered on hers, the candlelight bringing a softness to his eyes that she hadn't seen there before, and which threatened to put her off balance. Softness...in Trent Corbin? A seductive glow, more like!

Her eyelids fluttered under his. 'Mineral water, thanks.' He was bound to order wine with dinner and it would be wise to keep a clear head!

He nodded and ordered a Scotch for himself. As they pored over the dinner menu he said, 'This place is renowned for its fish. But anything they serve up is good.'

She took his advice and chose the fish of the day, with a smoked salmon dish as a starter. He chose a white wine to go with it.

Conversation was light and impersonal, until he asked idly, 'You have no boyfriend waiting for you back home?'

She glanced up at him. 'What makes you think that?' she said more sharply than she intended.

'You've made no attempt to contact him.'

'How do you know that?' she demanded indignantly, to hide a flutter of unease. 'You've been listening in to my calls?'

'You haven't *made* any calls...except for the ones you made for me in my office. There are three people in my house, Sandra, besides you. Not much goes unnoticed.'

Was that a warning? She swallowed, and eyed him steadily. 'I don't have a boyfriend...at the moment,' she said through almost gritted teeth. 'And my family and my flat-mate are all away...as I told you.'

She could almost read the words 'How convenient' in his eyes.

'What about the young man who was supposed to be touring down the coast with you?'

So he hadn't forgotten that flip remark of hers—a hasty improvisation at the time. 'Did I say it was a young man?' she hedged, and was vastly relieved when a balding man in a grey suit and loud tie approached their table.

He paused, almost bowing over Trent. 'Excuse me, but aren't you Trent Corbin?' he asked, his chubby face puckering in a smile. 'I recognised you from your pictures in the Press...and seeing you on TV.'

Trent looked up, a faint frown creasing his brow. 'If you want to discuss the resort...'

'Oh, no, no, it's nothing to do with that. I just saw you here and on the spur of the moment I——'

'If you've interrupted my dinner,' Trent sliced in over him, 'simply to have a pleasant chat...'

'Well, no...not really.' The man fingered his collar.

'Don't tell me...' Trent's mouth took on a heavily mocking slant. 'You're after my autograph!'

The man gave a nervous laugh. 'Well, only on a cheque, Mr Corbin.'

As Trent seemed to swell in his chair, his face darkening, the man said hastily, 'Sorry, I mustn't joke about it. Let me introduce myself...'

'I *am* here to have dinner,' Trent reminded him, his voice gratingly low, a warning light in his eye.

'Forgive me,' the man pleaded. 'I saw that you were between courses; I thought you wouldn't mind. I—I knew your father!'

'Ah.' Watching Trent, Sandra saw a marginal relaxing of his features. 'You were a friend of his?'

'Well, not a friend exactly...' The man straightened, his light brown eyes taking on a determined glint. 'My name is Lucas Elliott. I'm one of the directors of the Serenity Children's Home, just out of town. We provide twenty-four-hour care for children with intellectual and physical disabilities. Your father—Marshall Corbin—gave us a generous annual donation. We were hoping that you might continue...' He paused delicately.

'You mean you've interrupted a private dinner to ask for a *donation*?' Trent pierced the man with an icy glare. 'I don't discuss business matters in public restaurants!'

'Perhaps, Mr Elliott,' Sandra heard herself putting in gently, 'if you were to put your request in writing...'

Lucas Elliott beamed down at her. 'I shall, I shall. I just wanted to make myself known to you, Mr Corbin. In the hope that you might...that is...' He became flustered under Trent's cold stare. 'I thought the personal touch...'

'Oh, I get a lot of personal *touches*,' Trent said, laying scathing emphasis on the word. 'I could get buried under the avalanche of requests that come in. I can't promise anything,' he said curtly, dismissively. 'This is hardly the time or the place.'

'No, no, of course not.' But the man still hovered. 'Your father, Mr Corbin——' his voice dropped to a conspiratorial whisper '—was a fine man. A lovely man. So proud of his baby grandson. He told us he felt so blessed to have a bright, healthy grandson. That's why he gave so generously to *us* each year. Even after...' He looked at Trent's face and faltered. 'I know you have

lost your son, Mr Corbin, and I grieve for you, but——'

'You've done your cause no good, Elliott!' Trent's voice lashed over his. His face seemed carved from rock and his eyes were like slivers of ice. 'Now, are you going to leave or do I have to get someone to drag you away?'

The man's face blanched. 'I apologise, Mr Corbin! I'm truly sorry. I should never...' He backed hastily away. 'Please forgive me! I—I'll do as the lady suggests and put it in writing...'

'Don't bother!' Trent turned his back on the man, his hand closing round the glass on the table in front of him, his knuckles showing white. 'Insensitive money-suckers!' he muttered under his breath. He glanced at Sandra. 'And I don't need any lectures from you!'

Far from wanting to castigate him for his brutal dismissal of the man's appeal, as he seemed to be expecting, she felt a surge of sympathy for the anguish which she knew lay under the silver ice of his eyes. She reached across the table and covered his hand with hers.

'It's all right to be angry, Trent,' she said softly, knowing instinctively that his anger was only to hide his pain. 'It's all right to *feel*.'

He almost recoiled under her touch—or was it her words?

'He was wrong to approach you like that,' she added softly. 'But I suppose anguish makes you desperate.'

'Anguish?' He gave her a sharp look. 'What do you mean?'

'I mean Mr Elliott is a grieving parent, Trent, just like you. I know about the Serenity Children's Home; I visited it during my physiotherapy training. All the directors there are parents of disabled children. They give their children twenty-four-hour care, day in, day out, on a voluntary basis, relying solely on donations. It doesn't excuse what he did... but it does explain his desperation.'

Trent made no comment for a long moment. Whether he was letting it sink in or still angry and lost in his own grief she wasn't sure. But when he finally looked up again his eyes had lost their icy glitter.

'Do you want a dessert?' he asked, and his voice was quite different now, gentler. 'Or just coffee? They make a particularly good cappuccino here.'

'Just cappuccino will be fine,' she said, relieved that things were back to normal—at least on the surface. She gave a hidden sigh. Perhaps she would never know the extent of the agony that lay underneath.

'Thank you for a lovely dinner, Trent,' she said as they stepped into his house later. It was very quiet. The lights were low. Roland and Magda had obviously both retired. Suddenly she felt nervous. 'Well, goodnight,' she said brightly. 'I'll be off to bed, then.'

'Oh, surely... not yet.'

She paused, aware of a flutter in her chest.

'I thought you might like to take a look at the view from the tower,' Trent suggested. 'Assuming your ankle feels up to climbing stairs?'

'The tower?' she echoed, feeling faintly light-headed. Weren't his own private quarters up there somewhere? His *bedroom*? 'H-how can you see anything from up there at night?'

Was that thin, reedy sound her own voice? she wondered in disgust. Anyone would think she was afraid to be alone with him! She ought to be jumping at this chance to get closer to him... and maybe to his secrets.

'The clouds have all gone and there's a full moon... didn't you notice?' Trent's tone was gently mocking. 'Looking out over the sea from the tower on a moonlit night is a sight one shouldn't miss. I want to give others the chance to see that view too, which is why I'm planning a two-storey luxury hotel on this site.'

The reminder that he was building a tourist resort here, on the very spot where his house stood, taking in the land where *Harry's* house stood as well...it was like cold water being dashed over her. If Trent Corbin had any thought of seduction, she thought savagely, it was more likely to be seduction to his way of thinking, not into his bed!

'All right, then.' She gave in with a shrug. 'Show me your view. I'll be interested to see the tower, view or no view. It's a lovely old house,' she said pointedly.

'One that has served its purpose.' His tone had hardened, reminding her that sentimentality played no part in Trent Corbin's life.

As they passed through the lounge on their way to the stairs, she waved to a portrait over the fireplace.

'A relative of yours?' she asked.

'My father.'

Marshall Corbin. 'How would he feel about you pulling down his house?' she asked as Trent steered her towards the carpeted staircase.

'I'm sure he'd agree with me that you can't allow sentiment—or a pile of old stone—to stand in the way of progress.'

'Would he? You'll never know, will you?' she said on a sour note. And then, anxious not to alienate him, she added, 'Sorry. It's your house. Your business.' But Harry's house, she thought, is another matter.

'You like old houses, I gather?'

She glanced up at him, surprised that he should care about her views on the subject. 'Well, yes,' she said carefully. 'There's a lot of Australian history in old houses like this one...and the one next door.' *Harry's place*.

'One can't live in the past.' The harshness was back in his voice. Hearing it, she hastened on before he could dismiss the subject.

'No, but one can still be interested in it, surely? This house, for example. I imagine it's changed and developed quite a bit over the years. Do you know what it was like when it was first built? Do you know its history? How it evolved over the years?'

When he didn't answer straight away she thought he wasn't going to bother, that he wasn't interested, or perhaps didn't even know, didn't care. His hand gripped her elbow as they began to climb the stairs, with her using the rail for extra support. In the dimness of the stairwell his presence close behind her was raising the fine hairs at the back of her neck. Why is he bringing me up here? she wondered. She still wasn't convinced that it was simply to show her the view.

His voice at her ear, finally answering the question she'd asked, sent an odd little thrill through her.

'You're right, it's been converted, added to over the years. Originally it was a typical verandaed cottage, with an upstairs attic, not unlike Harry's next door. An early Victorian architect built on the two-storeyed hip-roofed pavilion and loggia, turning it into an Italianate villa—fashionable at the time. When my father retired and made this his permanent home, I added the tower at the junction of the two wings, designing it to suit the existing style.'

She flicked a look round at him. '*You* designed it?'

'I was an architect before I was a property developer,' he said, his tone as stonily impassive as his face.

'You were?' Pity you didn't stick to architecture, she was tempted to retort, thinking of the trouble Harry was in as a result of his change of course. 'More money, is there, in property development?' she asked nastily.

She sensed a sudden chill in the air. 'That's one way of looking at it.'

She heard the ice-hard cynicism in his voice and could have bitten out her tongue, sensing instinctively that his switch of career must have come around the time he'd

lost his wife and child. It was understandable that he would have felt the need for a change, a tough new challenge, to take his mind off his tragic loss, turning into a ruthless workaholic, a cold-hearted automaton, in his quest for forgetfulness, for something to fill the deep void in his life.

'But money wasn't the reason you went into it, was it, Trent?' she asked shrewdly, hoping to draw him out, hoping that he would say something to show that he wasn't as callous and uncaring as he'd led people to believe...that his heart wasn't as dead as Roland appeared to think. But was it for her own sake that she wanted to know...or for Harry's? she wondered with a faint tremor.

Trent paused as they reached the first landing, looking down at her for a moment, his eyes shadowed in the dimness. 'You think I do it simply for the satisfaction?' he mocked quietly.

She met his eye. '*Does* it give you satisfaction, Trent?' she asked quietly.

His lips moved, and for a second she thought he was going to answer her, even make some revealing admission. But as she watched his mouth slowly curved into a sardonic smile and he flicked his gaze away.

'That archway over there leads to my bedroom,' he said, and she gave a nervous gulp at the way his voice seemed to coil seductively around the word 'bedroom'. 'These stairs here...' he touched her shoulder, ushering her over to them '...lead to the top of the tower.'

She felt her cheeks burning. By the time they reached the room at the top of the tower she was quivering with a nervous, trembling expectancy.

Moonlight flooded the square room, which had windows all round. A low couch stood under one set of windows, elaborate stereo equipment under another. Trent didn't bother to switch on a light. It was bright enough—or more romantic?—without artificial light.

She felt his hands on her shoulders, guiding her over to the windows facing the ocean.

'How magnificent,' she breathed, but she was more aware of the man behind her than she was of the silvery beauty outside.

'You're trembling,' he murmured. His lips were so close to her hair that she could feel the fine strands parting under his breath. 'Are you cold?'

'I...' If she said no, he would wonder why she was trembling. If she said yes, what would he suggest to warm her? Already his hands were rubbing sensuously up and down her arms, sending tiny tendrils of delight curling through her. How could she feel the way she did, she wondered, when she despised the man—despised what he did to people—so much? 'I—I'm just panting a bit—from the climb up,' was her lame reply.

'Are you sure that's what it is, Sandra?' Now his lips were actually nuzzling into her hair, his breath warming the lobe of her ear under the parted strands. 'It couldn't be, could it, that you're as aware of me as I am of you?'

'Aware...of *you*?' She tried to inject scorn into her tone, but failed miserably, her voice sounding barely more than a croak.

'Why did you agree to come into my house, Sandra, in the first place?' he asked softly.

Alarm flared inside her. Could he have guessed? Did he suspect? Was that why he had brought her up here, why he was holding her like this in the romantic moonlight? Was he trying to weaken her, break down her defences, make her *confess*?

'I—I didn't have much choice,' she stammered.

'You could have demanded to be taken to a doctor...or to a hotel...' His lips dragged over her cheek, the roughness of his jaw scraping across the smoothness of hers. He still stood close behind her, his arms around her slender body, pulling her back against him. 'You felt the same challenge I felt, didn't you?' he breathed against

her cheek. 'You felt the electricity...the chemistry...whatever you want to call it.'

She sensed a jaded undercurrent, even under the velvety purr of his voice.

'I—I don't know what you're talking about,' she whispered, some power stronger than her own numbing her limbs, preventing her from twisting out of his arms.

'Don't play coy with me, Sandra. You want me as much as I want you.'

Her heart did a slow double somersault. She gave a soft, brittle laugh. 'You think so, do you? What gives you that idea?' She tried to sound derisive, but what came out was closer to a breathy whisper.

'Your kiss this afternoon told me. Your voice might have said no, but your lips, your body, your responses were all telling me the opposite.'

'You—you caught me off guard!'

'You still liked it. Loved it. Wanted more. Despite what you were telling me.'

He was right, damn him! And her body was crying for him now, despite all she knew about him, despite his callous disregard for her father, despite the kind of man he was...or had become.

As if sensing that he was making headway, he murmured, 'There hasn't been a woman in a long time that I've wanted as much as I want you, Sandra.'

She stiffened in his arms. 'And what Trent Corbin wants Trent Corbin must have?'

'I usually get what I want, yes.'

'You mean no woman has ever said no to you?' she asked, this time making a better job of sounding derisive.

'Oh, a number,' he said carelessly, as if it were of no consequence.

She stiffened. 'So you've had to *force* yourself on them?' she accused, her lip curling.

'I don't force myself on women, Sandra. If they say yes, well and good. If they say no... well, better luck next time.'

Such callous indifference! Such arrogance! She twisted her head round to give him a look of disdain. 'So you *don't* always get what you want?'

'Oh, I do when I want something badly enough,' he said, the smug note in his voice giving her a powerful urge to hit him. 'The women who've said no to me in the past were not worth losing any sleep over.'

'But women *have* said no to you?' she pursued sweetly. 'And you've left them alone?'

'That's right.'

'Then *I'm* saying no!'

He laughed softly, the sound sending shivers through her. 'Ah, but there's a difference in your case, Sandra. I *do* want you. Very much. And I know that you want me. You *will* give in, whatever you decide to say or do now. With you,' he breathed into the sensitive folds of her ear, 'it will be worth my while to take the time changing your no to a yes.'

'You'll be waiting!' Breathless as he made her feel, she still had some wits left. Yet she didn't seem capable of tearing herself from his arms.

'In the end I'll have you *begging* to come to me,' he taunted softly, the smile still in his voice. He rocked her gently in his arms. 'Fight it all you like, Sandra, but you will come to me... you will. And your reluctance now will make it that much sweeter.'

'Oh!' She had never come up against such flagrant arrogance, such mindless self-confidence, such *conceit*! If he had been any other man she would have laughed him out of her life.

So why wasn't she doing just that to Trent Corbin? Why did she feel as if her limbs were dissolving, turning to delicious, tingling liquid? Why was the blood

pounding through her body, an exquisite melting heat gathering in the pit of her stomach?

Was it simply the sexual challenge he was throwing at her? The lustful heat of a passion that could be quickly, easily satisfied? Or was this the start of something more? Something deeper, harder to ignore?

Whatever it was, she would die before she admitted to Trent Corbin how he made her feel!

She tossed her head, so that he was forced to draw back from his teasing plunder of her ear. 'You'll be waiting a long time,' she flung back in a breathless gasp. 'Because in a day or two I'll be out of your house and out of your life. And the answer will still be no!'

Then why, she found herself wondering in the same breath, did she feel so cold at the thought? So cold and yet so hot at the same time? Why did she feel this desolate, almost panicky sense of loss?

He had still made no move to release her. Why wasn't she tearing herself away from him? she berated herself in silent despair. Because fighting him would show him that he was getting to her? Reveal her desperation, her lack of control?

Or was it...she moaned silently...because she didn't *want* to tear herself away?

'A day or two will be all I'll need,' Trent drawled, 'to change your mind.'

She summoned her ebbing strength. 'Try your damned hardest! You just might be proved wrong for once! And if you t-try to force me,' she warned, 'I'll cry rape and— and ruin your life! You wouldn't want that, I'm sure!'

She caught her breath, appalled at what she'd said, expecting him to react violently to the threat, expecting his control to snap and the arms around her to hurl her away.

But instead he went still. And when he spoke his voice was low and steady. 'I won't be forcing you, Sandra. I won't need to.'

In her relief it was she who reacted violently, swinging savagely around and letting her fury spill out. 'Oh, you're so smug and self-confident, aren't you? You think no woman can resist you! *Ha*! Well, let me tell you, Trent Corbin, this is one woman who can. And will! I—I don't even *like* you!'

He didn't even flinch. 'You don't have to like me, Sandra.' He brought his hand up to cup her chin, and at once she realised her mistake in turning round to face him, feeling his fingers forcing her chin up until his lips were hovering just above hers. 'You only have to want me,' he murmured. 'As much as I want you.'

She stared up at him, weakness and desire fighting her will to crush him, wipe the smugness from his face. 'You—you think this is the way to get round me?' she whispered. 'Seducing me with soft words...mesmerising me with your potent manly spell?' She tried to sound mocking, in control, but she knew that any control she had left was fast slipping away.

Only the thought of Harry gave her the strength to keep on fighting him.

'You must be mad if you think liking doesn't need to come into it! That's just what I'd expect from you!'

'I'm just telling it how it is, Sandra. How it will be, when you come to me. I know you don't like me. I know you don't like a lot of the things I do. But you *do* want me. That's a good start.'

'How can you call it a start when I—when I *don't* want you and I never will?' she cried, knowing as she said it that it wasn't true.

'Then why are you still here?' he mocked. 'Why haven't you run away from this dire threat you say you don't want?'

'I—I don't run from anything!' she derided, defiance in the brave lift of her chin. 'I'm perfectly capable of *telling* you what I want—or don't want! And I—I expect you to respect my wishes!'

'Then why is it that your lips are saying one thing and your eyes quite another?' he taunted softly. 'Shall we just try it and see?' He brushed her lips with his.

She reacted as if he'd scalded her, jerking her head back, her eyes wild, like gleaming sapphires. 'Don't!' She twisted her head away. 'You're so wrong! You're so…insensitive! You know nothing about women, what they're really feeling or wanting. Not this woman, at any rate. I have to *like* a man before I can love him!'

'Love? I'm not asking for love,' Trent said, a faint chill in his voice now. 'I'm talking about desire. Passion. Need. *Wanting* someone. In my case, wanting a woman more than I've wanted anyone for a long time—maybe ever.' His eyes burned into her face. 'Having to have her.'

She couldn't look at him. *Wouldn't* look at him. Why was she even listening? 'Then you have the wrong girl,' she flung back hoarsely. 'I don't believe in sex without love,' she added tightly even as her body trembled, aching for him.

'That's rather old-fashioned, isn't it, for a sophisticated career girl in her—what—mid-twenties?' The corner of his mouth tilted. 'Are you telling me you've been in love with every man you've had sex with?'

He would never believe that she'd only had sex with one man, a man she had been wildly infatuated with at the time, believing that she *was* deeply in love. That was, until the scales had fallen from her eyes and she had realised the kind of man he was, that he was selfish and shallow, even in his lovemaking, and that, even if it had been true love she had felt for him, he was firmly against commitment.

'There *are* women—lots of women—who will only have sex with men they love, believe it or not!' she said scathingly. 'All women are not cold-bloodedly promiscuous.'

She managed to break free at last, and stepped resolutely away from him. But she didn't run, didn't flee the moonlit tower, tempted as she was to do so. She was determined to remain in control, shaky as she still felt. She moved over to the windows overlooking Kaoga Bay. Overlooking Harry's property, she realised.

She could see the shadowy outline of his cottage through the trees, the walls pearly in the moonlight. She sensed that Trent was moving closer, his panther-like tread barely making a sound on the polished boards. She felt him closing in on her, moving up behind...close behind...though this time he made no move to take her in his arms. But she could feel his body heat as he brushed against her, making the fine hairs at her nape spring upright.

She kept her eyes on Harry's cottage, thinking of Harry... thinking that the man standing behind her was the man who wanted to drive her father from his home, who had made veiled threats, who could even have resorted to vandalism.

Suddenly a light blinked on in Harry's cottage. Her heart rolled over. Wherever he had been all day, whatever pressures he was under, he was snug and safe in his home now.

Without consciously realising what she was doing, she sagged back against Trent, smiling her relief. As his arms closed around her she uttered no protest, made no move to stop him or shake free. Could Harry possibly have imagined the threats Trent had made? Misinterpreted something Trent or Roland had said? Maybe it *had* been children who had vandalised Harry's vegetable garden; maybe Trent *wasn't* the callous monster they both imagined him to be.

Dearly wanting that to be the case, she turned and smiled almost pleadingly up at him, all trace of the scorn and anger of a moment ago wiped from her face.

Only then did she see the way he was looking at her, and the breath stopped in her throat. He was looking at her not with tenderness, not with desire, not even with triumph, but with cold, hard suspicion!

'Wh-what is it?' she whispered. 'Why are you looking at me like that?'

'Your sudden about-face, Sandra, is mind-numbing,' he said, his voice as chilly, as remote as the look in his eyes. 'What did it?' he wondered aloud, his gaze flicking to the window, to the light through the trees. 'The sight of Harry Shaw's cottage? Now why, I wonder...?' His eyes snapped back to hers.

As she gulped nervously he pounced, snarling at her, 'Did *he* send you here? Did you and Harry plan this together...for you to inveigle your way into my house, hoping, maybe, that a little subtle seduction would bring me to my knees and get me off Harry's back? Oh, you're an expert at playing the tease, Sandra, at playing hard to get; you almost had me fooled!'

'No!' she cried, shocked that he should think she had set out to seduce *him*, for heaven's sake! 'Of course not! Are you crazy?' She felt a flare of shame as she hurled the denial back at him, because it *was* for Harry's sake that she had come here, it *was* with Harry's plight in mind that she had offered to help Trent in his office today, hoping to find some way to discredit him, and she *was* here in Trent's home under false pretences.

Should she tell him the truth, and throw herself on his mercy?

If Trent Corbin knew the word mercy!

For he'd never shown mercy to anyone before, as far as she knew. Why should he now? He looked dangerous, positively devilish in the ghostly moonlight. A lot of people said he *was* the devil. How was she to know how he might react? Especially now, while he was so angry.

Maybe tomorrow...after he'd calmed down a bit. And after she'd had a chance to slip over to see Harry and

let him know that she would be coming to stay with him. Because she would be out of Trent Corbin's house in a flash once Trent knew who she was.

Her heart quailed at the thought of telling Trent the truth. Admitting that she had lied to him. Or, at least, lied by omission.

She ducked away from him, covering her discomposure under a show of fiery indignation.

'Just because I *smiled* at you, don't get the idea I was ready to fall into your arms, or planning to seduce you, for pity's sake!' she said with withering contempt. 'What an insufferable ego you have!' Inspiration struck. 'And just as I was beginning to think you were ready to play the gentleman at last. *That* was why I smiled at you. And all you could do was—was *snarl* at me. And f-frighten me. Goodnight!' She wheeled round, taking care to favour her good leg. 'I'm going to bed!'

'Sandra, I'm sorry. . .' His hand shot out, closing over her wrist.

'Let me go!' she gritted, trying to inject ice into her voice. Her face was tight with rejection, but she was dismayingly aware that her body was quivering with anything *but* rejection.

'Damn it, Sandra, I don't say sorry often, but when I do I bloody well mean it!'

'All right!' Her cool control snapped. 'I accept your apology. *Now* will you let me go?' If he didn't she was afraid, desperately afraid, that she would fling herself into his arms!

Mercifully, his hand dropped away. 'I'll help you down the stairs,' he offered, his face taut.

'No need,' she gasped, limping hurriedly away from him. 'The hand-rail is all I'll need. Goodnight!'

'Goodnight, Sandra.' His words floated after her, his footsteps a dull echo behind her, solicitously close, but not too close.

All anger and suspicion had gone from his voice, she noted, her ears attuned now to any new inflexion. If anything, it had held a faintly baffled note, even a slight softening. If he had been anyone other than Trent Corbin, her father's enemy, a man known to pursue ruthlessly whatever he wanted, she might have melted under that softness and let him catch up with her...

CHAPTER EIGHT

'WELL, good morning, Sandra.' Trent glanced up from his newspaper as she came in to breakfast. 'We were letting you sleep in. Magda was going to bring your breakfast in to you later.'

'I'm not an invalid any more,' she almost snapped, tension gripping her at the sight of him. Despite herself her eyes lingered, mesmerised by his smooth, tiger-like grace as he rose to pull back a chair for her, by the attractive spikes of damp hair tumbling across his brow, by the tantalising V of bronzed flesh where his casual shirt lay open at the throat.

She had delayed coming down for breakfast, hoping that he and Roland would already have left for their trip down the coast. She'd been afraid that if he saw her Trent might have second thoughts about leaving her behind, alone in his house.

Roland was there too, wolfing down a huge plateful of steak and eggs. He barely glanced up as she stepped over to the table.

'You do seem to be walking better,' Trent observed. He spoke easily, as if nothing had happened between them the night before. 'You slept well, I trust?'

'Not all that well,' she admitted, adding as she caught him stifling a yawn, 'But obviously better than you did!' Looking closer, she noted that his morning shower and shave seemed to have done little to revive his heavy-lidded eyes or the dark smudges underneath, while the hard lines of his face looked more deeply etched than usual.

'Kind of you to notice,' he said in a wry tone, and surprised her by actually grinning—if that curving of his

117

lips could be called a grin. 'I dare say, even with the little sleep we both had, we still had more than if...' he paused, catching her eye and holding it '...the two of us had gone to bed earlier.'

Her cheeks flamed. Together, he meant! She hoped Roland was too busy feeding his face to catch on. She gave Trent a glowering look, wondering why *he* hadn't slept well. She knew why she hadn't. A jumble of fevered emotions, feelings of guilt and disbelief and dismay that she could feel the way she did about a man she ought to loathe and despise, had kept her tossing and turning for most of the night.

And the memories... Heart-stopping memories of Trent's arms around her, the way his lips had seared over her skin, her lips, her hair...the exquisite feelings that his closeness, his touch had stirred to life inside her.

Remembering again now, she gave herself a brisk shake, trying to blot out the turbulent images that filled her mind.

'Why don't you change your mind about coming down the coast with us this morning?' Trent said coaxingly as she helped herself to fruit and cereal.

She chewed her lip. For a second she was tempted. Why, she wasn't sure. Just to be with him? But Roland would be going too, and his presence would be a distinct dampener.

'No.' She shook her head. She had to go and see Harry. Had to let him know that she was here. 'I'll only be in the way.' Before he could assure her otherwise she added hastily, 'I'll be fine...really. I might go for a stroll in the fresh air later. I promise I'll keep away from the cliffs!'

She could feel Trent's eyes boring into her, could sense his mind ticking over—with suspicion? Mistrust?—and realised that she was holding her breath.

'Perhaps Roland should stay here and keep you out of harm's way,' he suggested smoothly. 'We don't want to risk any more accidents.'

'Roland?' That was the last thing she wanted! She glanced at the blond giant, hoping he would agree with her. But all he did was shrug. Of course... She compressed her lips. He would do anything Trent asked him to do—without question, no matter what he thought of the idea, how much he hated it.

'I don't need a babysitter!' She used a mixture of dignity and scorn to squash the idea. 'Besides, I can hardly get up to too much mischief,' she pointed out drily, 'with this ankle of mine.'

'It hasn't stopped you doing much so far,' Trent disagreed, his tone equally dry.

Her eyes narrowed. He *could* simply be referring to her walk along the cliff-top yesterday. Or to her climb up the stairs to the tower last night. But something told her—she gulped at the memory—that what he was specifically thinking of was her flight *down* the stairs later, when she had been fleeing the tower to escape him!

Her palms felt moist at the thought of it.

'Oh, you needn't worry.' Her tone was sarcastic. 'I promise not to run off with the family silver! I'm sure Magda will guard it for you.'

Trent reached indolently for another slice of toast. 'It's not the silver I'm worried about.'

She caught her breath. So he *was* worried about something. But what? Had he guessed she was hiding something from him? If he had, she'd be a fool to ask, and force him to admit it. She was finding it hard enough already to keep her identity a secret from him... and she had to! At least until Harry knew that she was here.

She'd be crazy to make any rash admissions before then. Trent Corbin was a heartless, ruthless man, a man who wouldn't take kindly to finding a spy in his house!

Because that was how he would see her, once he knew she was Harry Shaw's daughter!

Some spy, she brooded miserably. What have I found out that could possibly help Harry? Nothing! She thought of her father, distressed and under pressure from this man, and moistened her lips, knowing that this might be her last chance to find out more about Trent Corbin— and any dubious business practices he might be involved in.

'Anything you'd like me to do before I go out?' she offered, her eyelashes fluttering upwards. 'Any faxes to send? Letters you want typed? Calls to take?'

His eyes were hooded as they met hers. 'You won't be able to go into the office while I'm away. Magda's grabbing the chance to shampoo the carpet. And there's no need to answer the phone. I'll be leaving the answering machine on.'

She shrugged, hiding her unease. Had he arranged all this deliberately, to keep her from snooping? Didn't he trust her... after last night? Damn, she thought. Harry, I've failed you!

'However, there is one thing you can help me with before we leave,' Trent said as he rose from the table. 'I have some letters ready to post. Would you mind addressing and typing the envelopes for me?'

'Sure,' she said promptly—but not too eagerly. 'Do you want me to type the letters for you as well?'

'They're not actually letters, they're just handwritten slips—with an enclosure—that I want to slip into the envelopes when you've typed them. See you in my office. Don't rush your breakfast.'

He had the list of names and addresses ready for her to type when she joined him. A long list of societies and charitable organisations. She bit her lip, wondering what he had meant by 'an enclosure'. A curt, handwritten refusal? Surely he couldn't have meant... a *cheque*? For all these charities?

That'll be the day, she thought acidly—and was aware of a twinge of disappointment.

The last name on the list, she noted, her heart giving a tiny flip as she recognised it, was the Serenity Children's Home. She felt her spirits dive further. Was Trent sending them a refusal without even waiting for Lucas Elliott's formal request?

When she had finished typing the envelopes, rather than waiting for him to come out and collect them, she took them in to him. Her eyes widened as she saw a pile of cheques on his desk. The top one, she noticed, had a 'with compliments' slip attached, signed 'Trent Corbin'. It looked as if all the other cheques had similar slips attached.

Cheques . . . for all those organisations she'd typed envelopes for! Including the Serenity Children's Home!

Her heart soared, and she stifled a smile as Trent almost snatched the envelopes from her. 'Thanks, Sandra. I can finish them off now. I'll post them when I go out.'

His brow was faintly furrowed as he ushered her out. Because he suspected that she'd caught sight of the cheques? It was obvious that he hadn't wanted her to know about them, or surely he would have asked her to help him put them into their envelopes?

Was he afraid that she might spread it around that the hard-nosed Trent Corbin gave liberally to *charities*? Afraid that it would give people the idea that he was a soft touch, and lead to a flood of further requests? That it would spoil his image as a ruthless, tough-minded businessman, known to be untouched by sentiment?

She sighed. Trent Corbin was an extremely complex, puzzling, contradictory man. If only. . .

If only she could find out what the real Trent Corbin was like!

* * *

They'd gone at last. Sandra watched through her bedroom window as Trent's black Mercedes crunched over the gravel drive outside and disappeared through the trees. Pulling on a warm sweater, she left her room in search of Magda, bringing the walking stick for extra support.

She found the housekeeper in Trent's office, already moving furniture.

'Need any help?' she offered, pausing at the door.

'I can manage, thanks.' The housekeeper flicked her a brief smile.

'Well, if you're sure. I'm just going out for a stroll...OK?'

Magda waved a hand, as if whatever Mr Corbin's guests chose to do was of no concern to her.

This morning the skies were clear and the sun had more warmth. A gentle breeze barely ruffled the branches as she hastened through the trees towards Harry's house. Once there, she marched up the garden path and rapped on the front door.

To her frustration there was no response to her knock. With a sigh she headed for the back yard, hoping to find Harry there.

There was no sign of him. The back door, when she checked it, was locked, though a rear window was partially open, a flywire screen preventing flies from getting in, and she could see her father's car in the garage, so he couldn't have gone far.

His fishing gear and the spiked shoes he wore to go rock fishing, which he normally kept under the shaded veranda when he was at home, were nowhere to be seen. Almost certainly she would find him down in his private cove, rock fishing.

As she moved away from the house, she saw something flash out of the corner of her eye, as if the sun had glinted on something metallic, over in the low scrub and trees between Trent's place and Harry's. But when

she turned to look more closely there was nothing there. Nothing moved but the branches swaying in the breeze and a brightly coloured parrot that fluttered into the sky.

There's no one there, you idiot! Probably just a bit of broken glass catching the sun. Trent and Roland will be halfway down the coast by now. And Magda's busy cleaning carpets. Nobody's following you.

She quickened her pace, heading for the path that led down the steep slope into Harry's private cove, trying to ignore the faint twinges in her ankle each time she pressed her weight on her injured foot. She scrambled down the rocky path, almost sliding over the rocks and tufty scrub, until she reached the small stretch of sandy beach down below.

Waves were breaking over the rocks at either end of the cove, though not as dramatically as they must have crashed and thundered over these same rocks during the storm the other night. She sniffed the salt air appreciatively, her senses alive to the smells and sights and sounds...the thud and swish of the breakers on the beach, the bubbles of white froth swirling across the sand with each incoming wave, the tang of fine spray in her face from the waves breaking over the rocks. No wonder Harry loved it down here. His own private kingdom!

She frowned suddenly. Where was he? She couldn't see him anywhere! She narrowed her eyes, scanning the tumbled rocks at either end of the cove. There was no sign of him.

She felt a momentary qualm. Rock fishing was a dangerous sport. She'd warned Harry many times to be careful. But he'd always brushed aside her concern, insisting that he never took risks, that he always kept a close eye on the weather and the tides, that he knew the cove and its foibles inside out.

Then where was he? Crouched down among the rocks somewhere, so that she couldn't see him from down on the beach?

Using her stick to assist her, she trudged across the sand to the pile of rocks sheltering the cove on the ocean side of the bay, carefully picking her way over them. No Harry. With a sigh, she retraced her steps and headed for the rocks at the other end of the cove, climbing up and over them, her eyes leaping round.

Suddenly she froze, a hoarse groan escaping her lips. One of Harry's fishing-rods—she recognised it instantly—was wedged in between the rocks!

She stared at it for an endless, chilling moment. Harry *had* been here, but he certainly wasn't here now. Just to make sure, clinging to a dim hope, she scrambled around frantically, peering into every crevice, behind every rock, her heart sinking to her toes as she finally had to face the dreadful truth.

Harry had gone! The sea had swept him away...it must have! What else could possibly have happened? Preoccupied and stressed as he had been, with the pressure he was under to sell his home, he must have suffered a momentary lack of concentration, missed his footing, been caught by a wave, and then...

'Oh, no...oh, no...oh, Harry, no!'

She didn't realise she had uttered the words aloud until she heard a sharp voice behind her.

'What is it? What's wrong?'

It was *Trent Corbin's* voice!

She spun round in disbelief, the sight of him here in Harry's cove when he was supposed to be down along the coast somewhere—and the fact that he'd *followed* her down here—bringing all her pain over Harry and her fury at *him*, Trent Corbin, raging to the surface, spilling over in a reckless, explosive accusation.

'You're responsible for this! *You*, Trent Corbin! He's *drowned*, can't you see? And you're to blame! You're the one who made it happen!'

Trent advanced a step closer, his face hard, his eyes cold as flint. 'What the hell are you talking about?'

She raised her stick. 'Don't you come near me!' she shrilled, her body quivering, reacting of its own accord at the sight of him, even as her eyes widened in quick alarm.

He paused, his mouth twisting. 'For pity's sake, Sandra, I'm not going to hurt you. I just followed you to find out what you were up to. I had a feeling you were up to *something*.' His eyes pinned hers. 'And you're going to give me some answers ... now!'

'Not before you give me the answers *I* want!' she fired back, tearing her eyes away from his to point a trembling finger in the direction of the fishing-rod wedged in the rocks. 'Harry's *gone*! He's *drowned*!'

She spun back to face him. 'And you're to blame! Putting all that strain and pressure on him! You hounded him unmercifully, made him so stressed, so distracted he couldn't think straight, couldn't concentrate on what he was doing! And rock fishing needs all the concentration a man possesses!'

'You think ...' She saw comprehension dawning in Trent's eyes. But no softening. No wavering. None. 'I knew you were up to. something,' he grated, brushing aside her accusation. 'I had a sixth sense from the start. How could I have been such a fool as to trust you even as far as I did?' he berated himself, almost snarling. Jerking his head back, he rasped, 'So what's Harry Shaw to you?'

Their eyes clashed, his a dangerous silver, hers a stricken, piercing blue. 'He's my——' her voice choked '—he's my *father*!' What was the point in hiding it any longer? Harry was gone.

She saw the silver of Trent's eyes darken to glinting steel, and stepped back, frightened, as his frame seemed to swell with the sharp intake of his breath. 'Now why didn't that ever occur to me?' he ground out. 'Yes...that would explain a lot. Why you——' He twitched off the rest with a savage scowl. 'And you think something's

happened to him? Because you found his fishing-rod here on the rocks?'

As he waved a hand, the gold watch on his wrist flashed in the sun and she knew that that was what she had seen before. Trent must have been watching her search Harry's place, and then followed her down here, knowing that she wouldn't be on her guard because he was supposed to be on his way down the coast!

She tossed back her head, her golden hair catching the sun, a vivid, rippling wave. 'Of course something's happened to him! He was *fishing* here, and now he's not!' The words tumbled out in a ragged, breathless rush. 'He's been washed off the rocks and swept away by the tide and *d-drowned*!'

Suddenly her control snapped completely and she was pounding at him with her fists, lashing out blindly, scalding tears stinging her eyes. 'How could you per- secute a harmless, innocent man who only wanted to be left in peace?' she shrieked at him. 'If you wanted his land so desperately, why didn't you just——' she choked '—just burn it down?'

Strangled sobs racked her as she pummelled him, her despair over Harry stripping away all reason, all fairness, all feeling . . . deliberately wanting to hurt him as he'd hurt Harry, as *she* was hurting.

'Go on, say it!' Trent lashed back. 'Like I did before! With my wife and child in it!'

Through the fog of her misery and her anger it dimly penetrated that he was doing nothing to stop her hitting him; his lip was curled back from his teeth in a satanic kind of grin and he was taking her blows as if he welcomed them, as if he wanted her to hurt him. As if he wanted to be punished!

'I—I wouldn't be so cruel!' she gasped, her eyes blind with tears, her fists still lashing out wildly at his chest, his arms, his shoulders as if she didn't know how to stop.

Barely flinching under her blows, Trent bit back derisively, 'Other people are not so squeamish.'

'No? Maybe you *invite* their scorn, *invite* their doubts with the things you say and do!' she hurled back at him, beginning to wonder if she was going on hitting him just to get some reaction from him.

It took a moment before she realised that other hands were closing round her shoulders from behind, snatching her away, giant hands that lifted her off her feet as if she were no heavier than thistledown.

'Roland! Put her down!'

It was Trent's voice that rapped out, *his* hands that grabbed her this time as she tottered from Roland's slackened grasp.

'What the hell are *you* doing here?' Trent roared at the giant. 'I told you to take the car back to the garage!'

'I did take it back.' Roland stepped back a few paces. 'I came after you…in case you needed me. I'll stay over here,' he mumbled, 'in case she tries to get away.'

'Don't be a fool, Roland! She won't be going anywhere,' Trent said caustically. 'Not until I say so.'

'This isn't your property—and it never will be!' Sandra shrilled, using anger to hide a quick flare of alarm. 'If you think you'll be getting your hands on Harry's place now that he—now that he's out of your way, you can think again!'

Her golden hair swirled as she tossed back her head. 'I wouldn't sell to you if you were the last man on earth! Not after your treatment of Harry. And don't think the threats and scare tactics you used on my father will work with me; I assure you they won't!'

'And where——' Trent's voice dropped, deadly quiet now '—did you get the idea that I was using threats and scare tactics against your father? From Harry?' he demanded scathingly.

'Yes, from Harry!' she sneered, resorting to scorn as a shield against him. 'That's why I came down to Kaoga

Bay—because I was worried about him, fighting you all on his own. I wanted to help him. Give him some support. And—and now it's too late! Harry's——'

'I never threatened Harry,' Trent denied. 'And I don't use scare tactics.'

She drew in a quivering breath. She didn't believe him. Harry had told her that he had! Why would her father lie? 'And he—he told me how his vegetables had been dug up!' she flung at him. 'As if someone wanted to scare him off...dishearten him...drive him out. Who else would that be but you?'

'That was kids!'

'Was it?' She tilted her chin. 'Harry didn't think so. That's why I didn't tell anyone I was coming to Kaoga Bay. I wanted to make some enquiries for myself, on the quiet, without even telling Harry I was coming. I thought people would open up more—about *you*—if they didn't know I was Harry Shaw's daughter. I wanted to *help* Harry...do what I could for him.'

She lifted her chin a notch higher, looking Trent straight in the eye. 'He had a mild heart attack last year,' she said accusingly. 'I was afraid all the strain and pressure might bring on another one. I——' She bit her lip. 'I intended to contact him after I arrived, but...'

She shrugged, hastily changing the subject. 'I—I didn't actually ride all the way from Sydney, as I told you.' Her eyes fluttered away from his. 'I caught a train down to the nearest railway station and rode here from there. I wanted people to think I was just a cyclist passing through.'

'So that's what you were holding back,' Trent muttered as she finally paused for breath. 'Or *some* of it.' His very quietness made her shift nervously, scraping her feet on the rocks. 'And the friend who was coming down with you?'

She flushed. 'I—I just made that up to make you less suspicious—about me riding all the way down from Sydney alone.'

Trent drew in a long breath. 'You also came here to watch *me*, didn't you? To *spy* on me?' She could almost feel the dangerous vibes pulsing from him, the coiled-up anger simmering inside, and she involuntarily stepped back, out of his reach.

'And to do that,' he went on, his tone so quiet that she shivered, 'you had to inveigle your way into my home. How did you manage it?' he rasped. 'You risked letting me run into your deliberately?'

'Don't be mad! I didn't even know you were coming up behind me. It was pure luck.' *Luck*? She didn't feel so lucky now. *She* was the one standing in his way now, not Harry!

But overriding her unease was a deep misery at the way he was looking at her, at the disillusionment, perhaps even pain, that she could see in his eyes, hear in his voice.

She gulped nervously and looked up at him, meeting the eyes she had felt like drowning in only last night, feeling her bones weakening, even now, at the memory of his arm around her, of his lips in her hair, his warm breath blowing in her ear.

Did he still feel something for her? Did he, despite the vitriol she'd been hurling at him, despite her subterfuge in staying at his home under false pretenses, still want her, the way he had vowed last night that he wanted her, and must have her? Or had she wiped out all his desire for her?

Even in her despair over Harry she felt an overwhelming urge to wipe away the disillusionment and the anger that she saw in his eyes. If she could rekindle those feelings—even if they were only lustful feelings that didn't go deep—and convince him that her concern for Harry had overridden everything else, maybe he would forgive her for what she had done, and make allowances

for her, rather than looking at her the way he was now, as if he'd like to wring her neck!

Her heaping scorn on him, flinging reckless accusations at him about hounding Harry to his death, was only adding fuel to his anger.

She let her shoulders slump. 'I thought when you invited me into your—your home,' she whispered tremulously, stealing a look up at him, appealing to him with the full force of her blue eyes, letting the sunlight pick up and brighten their blueness, 'that here was my chance to—to find out more about you, maybe even find a way to stop you driving my father out of his home.

'When you talked so callously about the people you'd bought out and were so—so dismissive of that woman who brought a—a paternity suit against you I was sure the rumours about you must be true, and that you deserved whatever I could find out about you to—to use against you and...stop you. But I didn't count on...' she faltered, and flushed, flicking her tongue over her lips.

'Trent, I—it was wrong of me to blame you for—for whatever has happened to Harry.' She took a deep breath and added in a rush, 'I don't think you're the heartless monster you like to make out!'

For a long, endless second the air throbbed between them. She held her breath, her face pale and strained. Trent's voice finally broke the awful tension, the harsh lines of his face easing, his eyes losing their ice-hard glitter.

'Your concern for your father is understandable, Sandra. It...explains a lot.'

She bit her lip. 'I—I'm sorry I flew at you before. It came as such a shock, finding Harry's fishing-rod on the rocks. Wh-whatever's happened to him, I'm sure it was an accident. Rock fishing is terribly dangerous. I was always warning him to be careful. It must have been

a——' her voice broke '—a rogue wave that caught him and swept him off the rocks!'

'Let's not look on the black side yet.' Trent touched her arm. 'There may still be some other explanation. Your father's no novice, and I've seen the sea much wilder than it is today. Let's get back up to Harry's place so I can take a look around... I have an odd feeling about this.'

She nodded miserably, sure that he was just trying to raise her spirits. She let him take her arm and help her down off the rocks and up the steep slope, a tight-lipped Roland standing aside to let them go up ahead of him. She could feel the giant's hot glare on her back and knew that she hadn't endeared herself to him for hurling accusations at his boss.

Trent tried to calm her fears for Harry on the way up, and she made a supreme effort to blot out for now all thought of what might have happened to him, so that she was really only conscious of Trent's strong arm pinning her to his side, the warmth of his body against hers, his face a mere breath away from hers.

It was as if she belonged there, close to him. Belonged in his arms. Which was crazy. How could she feel so strongly for a man she'd known for so short a time, a man she had been hurling abuse at only moments ago, a man she had mistrusted up until now, and still didn't know nearly enough about?

She dragged her thoughts back to Harry, gulping down a sob as they neared the top of the cliff. 'He's not at home,' she moaned aloud. 'I looked. He's d-drowned... I know he has!'

Trent's hand gave her arm a comforting squeeze. 'Let's not panic yet. Let me take a look around; it won't take a minute.'

She nodded mutely, some instinct, some sixth sense, telling her that Trent was trying his best to help her...that

if he could find something at Harry's that would set her
mind at rest he would.

Was she being hopelessly naïve and trusting? And what
did it say about *her*...that she could put her trust in
the one man in the world least likely to be trustworthy,
a man whose uncaring, ruthless attitude to other people
made him the last man on earth she should ever trust?

Only a woman helplessly in love would trust so blindly
and so foolishly.

Her body tensed in disbelief. No, she thought. That's
impossible! It's crazy! Her foot stumbled on a loose rock,
and she would have fallen if Trent's arms hadn't been
securely holding her.

'I—I nearly went over on my ankle,' she hastily
explained, knowing that he must have felt her tense up
before she'd stumbled, and hoping he would put it down
to a fleeting unsteadiness. 'It's all right, I——'

'Put your arm round my neck!' he commanded, and
when she did he hauled her the rest of the way up with
her feet barely touching the ground.

He paused at a rustic seat at the top of the cliff, overlooking the bay.

'Look, why don't you rest here for a moment and then
start walking slowly back to my place? I'll follow in a
few minutes. If necessary, we'll call in the police then.
Roland, you stay with her, will you? And give her a hand
on the way back.'

The thought of Roland's hands on her brought an instant, horrified protest to her lips. 'I can walk without
any help now that we're on level ground!' She unwound
her arm from round Trent's neck and demonstrated,
planting both feet firmly on the ground and taking a few
equally firm steps. Even if her ankle had caused her the
most agonising pain she wouldn't have so much as
winced.

Luckily, it didn't feel too bad. But the thought of
resting it briefly before heading back to Trent's house

and facing up to the trauma of swarming police and a barrage of distressing questions sounded heavenly. She was sure that Trent wouldn't find anything, but she was grateful to him for trying...even though she suspected that it was only to comfort her. The fishing-rod she'd found down in the cove was too ominous a sign to keep her hopes alive any longer.

Harry was gone. She would simply have to face up to it. How it had happened, whether it had been an accident, a rogue wave, a heart attack or—her heart quailed—even suicide, heaven forbid, was something she preferred not to think about just now.

It hadn't sunk in yet, but she knew it would, in time...once Trent was forced to admit that there was no other explanation.

Facing Roland, she said firmly, 'You go with Trent and help him look around. I'll be fine,' she promised Trent.

'Roland, you'll stay with her,' he insisted, and the giant nodded dutifully.

Sandra hid a grimace. 'Just don't be long!' she muttered as Trent swung away.

CHAPTER NINE

SANDRA sank down on the rustic seat, finding that it *was* a relief to put her foot up. Roland hovered over her but she ignored him, her gaze following Trent as he strode off, her senses, even in her misery, alive to every detail of him—the powerful breadth of his shoulders, the tapering line of his back, the tiger-like grace of his hips.

She had misjudged him. He wasn't the unfeeling devil she had imagined him to be. She had let his ruthless pursuit of Harry's property blind her to his good points... and he had many of those, she was discovering more and more.

She had built him up in her mind as a villain, a cold-hearted devil, and in many ways he was. But to deliberately hound Harry to the grave, to viciously vandalise his property... No! She had stopped believing that he would go to such dire lengths to get his hands on a property he wanted.

Was she being naïve? Listening to her heart rather than her head? Had she only stopped believing the worst of him because—she felt a tingling in the pit of her stomach, recalling his kisses—because she was falling *in love* with him?

She gave a trembling sigh. Was that really what was happening? Could it happen so quickly, strike so suddenly? There was so much about him that she still didn't know, still didn't approve of, still didn't altogether trust. Those threats Harry had said he'd made, for instance. Trent had denied making them... but why would Harry lie?

Despite all that, she had caught glimpses of what lay below the hard, unfeeling shell that Trent had wrapped around himself, the callous façade that he liked the world to see. Much as he might want Harry's land, he would never wish any harm to come to her father, she was sure of it. She had been wrong to hurl those vicious accusations at him.

She had been looking for someone to blame for whatever had happened to Harry and Trent Corbin had fitted the bill to perfection. The property shark, the cold-hearted predator who preyed on his victims, sweeping aside anyone who stood in his way. It had been easier to blame him than to believe that a simple, tragic rock-fishing accident—a freak wave, rolling in and dragging out to sea any fisherman in its way—could have taken Harry from her.

How often had she read such stories in the papers? It happened. Often. It had happened to Harry. She had to face it.

A tear welled up and rolled down her cheek.

'It's too bad about your father.'

She blinked, and glanced up to see Roland's pale eyes gleaming down at her.

'You were wrong to blame Mr Corbin.' A shadow darkened his brow. 'He's a good man. And he's doing all he can to help you!'

His voice throbbed with resentment. She sensed that it annoyed and pained him that she had attacked his boss, that she could have accused him of hounding a man to his death.

She heaved a sigh. 'He hasn't done a whole lot in the past to gain a person's trust,' she pointed out quietly, hoping to draw him out.

'You know nothing about him!' Roland balled his great hands into fists. 'He's nothing like people make out he is. People who *know* him see the good in him,

and the good he does. Not that *he* cares what people think of him.'

'What good does Trent do?' she challenged, silently urging the giant to open up a bit more about Trent. She knew so little about the man underneath! If he wasn't as unfeeling, as uncaring as people made him out to be—as he himself liked people to think—she wanted to know what the real Trent Corbin was like. 'He doesn't strike me as being a man who even *has* feelings,' she ventured, 'let alone a man who cares about other people!'

'How would you feel,' Roland sneered, 'if you'd lost your loved ones in a fire and blamed yourself for it? They say it took four strong men to stop him plunging into that inferno. As it was, he suffered such bad burns to his hands, trying to force his way in, that he needed skin grafts!'

She felt a lump rise to her throat. She had noticed Trent's hands, and had put their odd colour down to a skin complaint of some kind. Skin grafts...of course. She should have guessed.

'Then why were there those ugly rumours afterwards?' she wondered aloud. People could be so blind, she thought, so cruel! And she was just as guilty, for giving credence to the rumours.

'Why?' Roland echoed derisively. 'Because he *wanted* people to blame him. Because he blamed himself, and he still does. To a man like Mr Corbin, showing off his burns and his grief would have been taking the easy way out. He never looked for sympathy, never wanted it.'

'How do you know all this, Roland?' she asked. 'Were you with him back in those days?'

'If I had been there wouldn't have been any rumours,' he flung back with scorn. 'No, I wasn't there, but Magda was. She's been with the family for years. And I've seen and heard things since I've been with him. There was the day my——' He flicked her a sharp look. 'Did he tell you about my wife?'

'He told me your wife was overseas,' she said slowly. Her eyes wavered. 'You're going to tell me he paid for her holiday?' She shrugged. 'Oh, well, I dare say he could afford it!'

'Holiday?' Roland's voice sharpened. 'He told you it was a *holiday*?'

'Well, I just assumed... Wasn't it?'

'Hardly. My wife needed an urgent life-saving operation that could only be done in America. There was no way I could raise that kind of money. I tried everything short of begging.' A glint of pride glowed in the pale eyes. 'We didn't own the house we lived in, or even own a car, or I'd have sold those. I was desperate.' Raw emotion roughened his voice. 'I didn't know what to do.'

'So Trent offered to help?' As she asked the question, an image of Trent's face rose in her mind, and she saw again the hard, uncompromising lines, the ruthless mouth, the ice-cold eyes... devil's eyes that barely softened, even in the heat of passion. Was there a vastly different Trent Corbin behind the cold, uncaring, rigidly controlled property tycoon that most people saw?

'It... wasn't as simple as that.' Roland's shoulders hunched as he shifted restlessly. 'Mr Corbin didn't even know me then. I was just a labourer on one of his building sites. He only heard about me... about my wife's illness... because I—I did something stupid. Wrong. Bad.' His eyes slid away.

'Bad?' she echoed.

He sucked in his breath. 'I stole some stuff from the site,' he growled. 'Building materials I thought nobody would want—or miss. I sold them. And was found out. The foreman gave me the sack. Mr Corbin heard about it and came to see me. Somehow he'd found out about my wife's illness and he... he gave me a second chance.'

Roland went on huskily, 'He offered me this job down here, looking after this place and the other headland

properties he was buying up. In return he said he'd send
my wife to America for her operation. He even sent me
over there with her, and let me stay with her till she was
out of danger and her sister—with help from Mr
Corbin—was able to join her.'

'And she's going to be all right?' The wind spread
threads of golden hair across her face but she barely
noticed. This hardly sounded like the cold-hearted Trent
Corbin she'd heard such harsh things about—that he
liked to make out he was. A lot of bosses, she mused,
would have scrubbed their hands of a man who had
stolen from them. She would have put Trent Corbin into
that category.

Roland nodded. 'My wife will be home soon, good
as new.' For the first time she saw a real softening in
the pale, close-set eyes. 'Mr Corbin says we can both
stay on here until his house is ready to be demolished.
Then he'll find me some work back in Sydney or somewhere else. He says the Nissan Patrol is mine to keep.
He's a generous man, through and through.

'I've been saving hard since I've been down here,' he
added gruffly. 'Saving for a house of our own. I could
never have done that without Mr Corbin's help.'

'You've been very fortunate, Roland.' What would
have happened to him, and to his wife, Sandra wondered, if Trent hadn't given him that second chance?
'And I must admit I'm surprised at Trent's…humanity,'
she admitted. 'I suppose he's kept quiet about what he
did for you,' she added musingly, 'because he doesn't
want people to see him as weak—for giving you a second
chance.'

'Everybody knows he's not weak,' Roland scoffed.
'He's always tight-lipped about the good things he does.
And he insists that the people who know about it keep
quiet too. I bet you've never heard about the nursing
homes he's built either, or the shelters for the homeless,
or the charities he gives generously to? He gets floods

of requests; he can't give to all of them, but you'd be surprised at how much of his money he gives away.'

'A lot of people would suggest that he gains generous tax benefits,' she murmured, but she made the suggestion half-heartedly, not wanting to think of Trent giving donations to charity for what he could get out of it. She might have believed it once, but not any more. And he certainly couldn't be doing it for any personal glory or publicity. He'd tried to hide his donations...even from her!

'Think what you like.' Roland's lip curled. 'You think he cares what you or anyone else think of him? He just does things for people...on the quiet. That's his way.'

'You call forcing people out of their homes *doing* things for people?' she asked quietly, thinking of Harry, and all the others before him, wondering how Roland would defend him for *that*.

'Mr Corbin never tried to *force* your father out,' Roland sneered. 'If you want my opinion he was *too* considerate, *too* patient with him. He made Harry a ridiculously generous offer. If Harry had taken it, instead of holding out for more, he might be alive today.'

She stiffened. 'What do you mean?' she asked sharply.

'I mean,' Roland growled, 'that he could have been living in a brand-new house by now, down along the coast somewhere, safe and sound, instead of hanging around those dangerous rocks down below and getting himself drowned!'

'Oh.' She shivered. For a chilling second she had wondered if the giant, eager to repay his debt to Trent Corbin, could have taken matters into his own hands.

'So...' Roland leaned over her, his big frame blocking out the warm rays of the late-morning sun '...what will you do with Harry's house? You realise it's yours now. You will sell, won't you—now that he's gone? So that Mr Corbin can build his resort?' She could feel his hot breath on her face.

'Sell?' She frowned up at him.

'*You* don't want Harry's house.' A gust of wind lifted his blond hair as he loomed over her. 'Or his land. You'll be a rich woman if you sell. Mr Corbin will make it worth your while.'

She snapped angrily, 'We don't even know for sure that Harry's d-dead!' Her heart gave a sick lurch. 'Did Trent Corbin put you up to this?' she hissed at him. She swung her legs off the seat, bracing herself to leap up, looking for a way to duck past him as she did so without tumbling over the cliff in the process!

'Of course not. But you know it's what he wants.' His hands shot out to grip her arms. 'All you have to do is promise to sell!'

'Let go of me!' Not for the world would she let him see how nervous she suddenly felt. As she struggled to get up he obliged by clamping his hands more tightly round her arms and hauling her up, almost lifting her off her feet. She was alarmingly aware of the cliff-edge only a step or two behind them.

'Go on...promise!' He shook her.

A voice lashed out from behind them, '*Roland*! What the hell do you think you're doing? Let her go!'

It was Trent's voice! As she sagged in relief, Roland's head whipped round, his hands dropping from her arms as if they were suddenly red-hot.

'Mr Corbin!' he bleated, his great shoulders slumping. 'I was just—I was asking if she would sell Harry's place...now that he's gone! I wasn't going to——'

'Don't you ever touch her again!' Trent almost knocked him flying as he lunged between them, his face a black mask of fury. 'You keep away from her! You understand?'

Roland teetered back, one of his great feet almost slipping over the cliff-edge. 'I wasn't going to hurt her, Mr Corbin! I swear it! I was just——'

'Just threatening and intimidating her!' Trent roared at him. His eyes narrowed to silver slits. 'The way you threatened and intimidated Harry?' he roared, causing the giant's eyes to slide away. '*Hell*! I've been a bloody fool, believing your lies...*trusting* you!'

'Mr Corbin, I never laid a finger on Harry!' croaked the giant, regaining his balance. 'I'd never hurt a fly! You know that, Mr Corbin!'

'You think threats don't hurt people?'

'I was doing it for *you*, Mr Corbin!' Roland spread out his great hands in agonised appeal.

Trent gave a muffled curse. 'It's nothing to do with you!' His voice flayed the giant. 'Get out of my sight! You've just worked your last day for me! I'll see you back at the house!'

'Sure, boss, sure!' Roland stumbled past him. 'If you want me to go, I'll go. You done enough for me and my wife to last us a lifetime!' He scuttled off, his head bowed, moaning over his shoulder, 'I never would have hurt her! *Or* Harry. Never in a million years! You gotta believe me!'

Sandra found herself feeling almost sorry for the anguished giant.

Trent spun round, gathering her in his arms. 'Are you all right?' He peered into her face.

She drew in a quivering breath, feeling weak at the concern, the anger, the warmth, to say nothing of the other emotions that she couldn't read so easily but which she could see chasing across his eyes.

'Sure. I'm fine.'

'If he'd hurt you,' Trent grated, 'I would have killed him!'

She stopped breathing. What was he saying? Did he simply mean that he felt responsible for her while she was under his roof? Or was he thinking of the scandal if it got out that his burly sidekick had been roughing

her up, intimidating her, to get hold of a property he wanted?

Or could it be that he...? No! That was ridiculous! Wasn't it?

She found her voice, injecting a bantering note into it to cover her confusion, her uncertainty. 'I guess it wouldn't have done the reputation of your future resort much good—I mean if people found out that the man who works for you used rough-arm tactics to get hold of a property you wanted.'

'To hell with the bloody resort!' Trent exploded. 'I'm starting to rue the day I ever dreamed it up. It was you I was thinking about. Just you!' His fingers dug into her shoulders, his eyes scorching into hers. 'You're sure you're all right?'

She stared up at him, nodding, feeling sightly dazed as she sensed his concern—for *her*. Not for himself. Not for his reputation—for *her*.

And then she remembered Harry.

'D-did you find anything?' she whispered, despair sweeping over her, convinced that any hope was futile.

'Sandra, I want you to come with me.' He tugged her away from the cliffs, in the direction of Harry's cottage. 'I don't want to raise your hopes too much, but one thing I am sure of is that Harry didn't go fishing down in that cove this morning.'

Her lips parted, her heart leaping to her mouth. 'How—how do you know that?'

'I found Harry's fishing gear and his spiked boots in his garage, carefully hidden under his car.'

'Hidden?' She gaped at him. 'But why——?'

'Come with me. I want you to see for yourself, not take my word for it.' A muscle flicked at the edge of his jaw.

Did he still think she didn't trust him? 'Trent, I believe you!' Any threats made to Harry, she realised now,

had been made on Roland's own initiative, in the misguided belief that he was helping Trent. Without Trent's knowledge. But Roland, she was sure, wasn't a violent man. He would never have harmed Harry—*or* her.

'Trent,' she ventured as he ushered her round Harry's cottage to the back yard. 'I'm sure Roland had no intention of hurting me. What he did was stupid, and a bit scary, but I don't want him losing his job over it.'

As she saw his face tighten she hastened on. 'I'm sure he's learnt his lesson. He was just trying to do something for *you*, Trent. He's so grateful to you for what you did for his wife...'

She felt him flinch. 'He promised he wouldn't tell anyone about that!'

'Trent, he *worships* you. He'd do anything for you. He just went a bit overboard, that's all, because he wanted so much to help you in return...help you get your resort.'

Trent scowled. 'I don't want his gratitude. Or his worship. And I certainly don't want that kind of help. All I ever wanted from him was his loyalty and his obedience. And his silence. I made it a condition when I sent his wife overseas that he kept his mouth shut about it.'

'It's not so easy keeping quiet about things that mean a lot to you,' she said quietly. 'Please, Trent...don't be too hard on him.'

He paused halfway across the yard and looked down at her. 'You're a compassionate girl, Sandra,' he said roughly, his hand tightening round her waist. 'And far too forgiving. Most women would have been baying for his blood.'

'I think *you're* more compassionate, Trent, than *you* make out you are,' she breathed, and felt his body stiffen. 'Admitting it is not a weakness,' she told him softly.

'Any feelings are a weakness,' he growled, and she sighed, feeling the deep chasm that still lay between them, even held close to him like this. She could feel him slipping away from her again, emotionally.

He's still suffering, still torturing himself over what happened to his family, she thought bleakly. Still blaming himself, still angry, still far from being at peace. That's why he keeps such a tight rein on his deepest emotions, why he pretends not to care about people, why he's so driven to achieve more and more. He's trying to forget . . . to blot out the pain.

And he throws himself into his work to give his life some meaning, some purpose. But it hasn't given him what he's been looking for. He's still a tortured soul, hitting out at the world in his hurt and self-blame.

'You're thinking of your wife and child, aren't you?' she whispered, feeling his agony and wanting to reach out to him. 'Trent . . .' She looked up at him. 'You have to stop blaming yourself for what happened. You didn't burn down that house deliberately. It was an accident . . .'

He reacted violently, his head jerking back. 'It should have been me that died, not them,' he choked out, his voice a ragged rasp. 'I should have been protecting them. Who else can I blame? I was the one who lit that fire. I was the one who relied on that flimsy screen. I was the one who waltzed off to safety and left them to perish in their own beds!' It came out in a bitter rush, raw grief in his eyes, self-disgust in the lift of his lips.

'Trent——'

'It was *my* fault!' he sliced over her. 'And now I have to live with it. That's my punishment . . . a just punishment.'

'Oh, Trent, do you truly think your wife would have wanted you to go on punishing yourself like this?' Now that he had exposed his anguish, admitted it, would he listen to her? 'Would you have wanted her to go on suf-

fering and punishing herself forever if *she* had been the one to survive and you the one to die?'

When he remained tight-lipped she pressed home her point. 'You would have wanted her to find happiness again, wouldn't you? And peace?'

'Leave it, Sandra,' he said wearily. 'My wife and I were different people. What I might want for her would never work for me. How can I ever find happiness, or peace? It's impossible. I have nothing left to give.'

She steeled herself not to despair, and even more so not to show pity. 'You mean you're *scared* to feel in case it hurts again,' she challenged, wanting him to face it, admit it.

'Damn it, Sandra, I said leave it!'

She lifted her chin, defying him, her blue eyes as vivid as the sunlit sea. 'Roland says you do care about people . . . you just won't admit it, won't let people know about the things you do.'

His brow plunged. 'What's he been saying to you?'

'Oh, just defending you, assuring me that you're not the callous monster most people think you are. That you do good things for people. Trent, I've *seen* some of the good things you do. You tried to hide those cheques you were sending out this morning but I knew what they were for.'

His jaw clenched. 'I can do things for people without giving a piece of myself,' he rasped. 'As for letting people know what I do, a man would be a damned fool to publicise it. When people know you do things they take advantage of you!'

She almost smiled, not fooled for a minute, knowing instinctively that fear of being taken advantage of wasn't the reason why he kept quiet about what he did. Not wanting to give a piece of himself was much closer to the mark.

'So you're going to let people go on thinking you're the devil incarnate, without a caring bone in your body,' she said with a sigh. 'And you're not going to give anyone a chance to get close enough to you to find out if you *can* feel again.'

The brief silence that fell between them throbbed with a breathless tension. Just as she thought he was about to withdraw from her again, perhaps even fling her away from him, she saw his lips lift in sensuous invitation, a glint of pure silver in his eyes.

He brought his hands up to close over her shoulders. 'I'd like to get close to *you*, Sandra,' he said in an entirely different voice—a deep, seductive purr that set her nerve-ends screaming. He was saying nothing about feelings, she noted, a hot ache growing in her throat, but as she felt her body stirring under the brush of his fingers over her shoulderblades she thought, with a fierce yearning, that maybe...maybe...in time...

Some powerful inner force impelled her to reach up and put her hand to his cheek, and to say lightly, gently, 'It looked to me a few moments ago as if you did have feelings, Trent. When you thought Roland might have hurt me.'

He lifted a hand and put it over hers. 'Oh, I have feelings all right,' he muttered, brushing his lips over hers, tasting their softness. 'Every time I touch you...every time you touch me. I want you, Sandra. I want you more than I've wanted any woman since...' His mouth twitched the rest off. He still couldn't say it, couldn't even say her name! 'You know I want you!' he growled against her parted lips.

She sighed, her body trembling. He wanted her, but he would never love her, never allow himself to feel for her what he had felt for his wife. Because he saw love, feelings, as a weakness. And it was obvious that he was never going to let himself be that vulnerable again.

'You'd better show me . . . what it is you want to show me,' she said with a sigh, reluctantly drawing back, out of the enticement of his arms, feeling suddenly ashamed that for the past few minutes she had entirely forgotten about Harry.

CHAPTER TEN

TRENT let his hands drop away. 'Over here,' he said, and led Sandra across the yard towards Harry's garage.

There was no doubt about it. It was Harry's fishing gear. Harry's spiked boots. He never went rock fishing without them.

'And there's something inside the house I'd like you to see as well,' he said, steering her to the back door. 'I climbed in a window before. But this time we can go in this way.' He tugged open the back door.

'It was locked before!' she cried. 'Where did you find the key?'

'Hidden in the kitchen. Harry must have locked the back door from the inside and gone out the front way.'

She followed him in. 'Well . . . what did you find?' she demanded, glancing round. The kitchen looked unusually neat. No food or dirty dishes left lying about. No mess.

'In here.' He led her into Harry's bedroom. 'Take a look at the lamp. The lamp *cord*, rather.'

Her gaze followed the lamp cord down to a square box on the floor, partially hidden by the curtains at the window.

'A timing device!' she cried. She glanced at Trent. 'You think that—that Harry wasn't at home last night when we saw that light come on in his house? That he'd *set* it to come on—to make people think he *was* at home?' She bit her lip in confusion. 'I don't——' She broke off, her head spinning round. 'Did you hear something?'

Trent held up a hand. 'Shh!'

'Roland?' she whispered. Had the giant followed them here instead of going back to Trent's? Hoping that Trent might have cooled down a bit by now?

'He wouldn't dare. He'll be waiting for me at home where I told him to wait.' Trent touched her arm. 'You stay here.'

He strode out. As she started to follow, she heard a shout, and scuffling sounds. Eyes widening, she snatched up a paperweight from the desk and flew out, in time to see Trent stagger back against the wall. A man in a raincoat and cap, bellowing abuse, was pounding him with his fists.

'You bloody vulture, Corbin! I might have known you'd try something like this! If you've wrecked any-thing——'

'*Harry*!'

Her shriek stopped the pounding as if by magic. The man's fists froze in mid-air, his head whipping round.

'Alex! What are *you* doing here? And what are you doing with *him*?' Harry's eyes, the same bright blue as her own but crinkled by the sun, pierced hers. 'Don't tell me Corbin's been trying to get at *you* now—having failed to browbeat me? Hoping he could get you to talk me round, was he? The mongrel!'

'Harry, where have you *been*?' she croaked. 'We thought something had happened to you! We thought you'd *drowned*!'

'Drowned? Oh, hell.' Harry gave a sheepish grin. 'So someone found that fishing-rod I planted, did they, and couldn't wait to drag you down here to get all the wrong ideas?' He shook his head. 'The last thing I wanted was to drag you into this, love.'

He flicked a virulent glance at Trent. 'I suppose *you* were the one who found it, were you? I might have guessed you or your henchman Roland would come nosing around my place before I had a chance to get

back. And as soon as you thought I was dead, you shark, you decided you'd start work on my daughter, did you?'

His eyes snapped back to Sandra. 'How did he find you? You're meant to be up in the Blue Mountains somewhere, love, out of contact. I thought you'd be safely gone for a week!'

'*Safely* gone?' she echoed, with a bewildered shake of her head.

'Look.' Harry heaved a sigh. 'I just wanted to slip quietly away for a few days without anyone knowing I was gone. I reckoned my place here wouldn't be safe if you, Corbin—or your thug Roland—knew I'd gone away. So I left my car at home and a window partly open and hid my fishing gear to make it look as if I was still at home. And I set up lights to come on at night.'

'A master stroke, Harry,' Trent applauded as he paused for breath.

Harry ignored him. 'And as a last resort I planted that fishing-rod down in the cove. To put you off the scent, Corbin, in case one of you *did* start nosing around. I didn't want you guessing I'd gone away and deciding to do some damage to my place in my absence. If you thought I'd been swept out to sea, and called in the police, so much the better. They'd have looked after my place till I got back!'

He swung back to face his daughter. 'But I never meant *you*, love, to——'

'What's this all about, Harry?' Trent sliced in, his eyes narrowed. 'You just wanted to take a holiday—was that it? Or have you been . . . up to something?'

Harry's lips curled in a sly grin. 'You'll find out.' He stuck out his jaw. 'When you left Kaoga Bay after making that last big offer of yours, Corbin, that's when I grabbed my chance. Like I said, I arranged it so that your beefy offsider would think I was still at home. I didn't trust him . . . or *you*. I might have guessed you'd show up again, Corbin, before I got back!'

'We never would have realised you'd gone away, Harry,' Trent commented, his face grimly impassive, 'if your daughter hadn't come down here to offer you some moral support—and panicked when she found you missing and your fishing-rod down in the cove.'

'Oh, hell. I'm sorry, love.' Harry reached for his daughter's hand. 'Why didn't you tell me you'd cancelled the Blue Mountains trip and were coming down?'

She sighed. 'I wanted a couple of days to talk to the people in the town...and to find out more about——' she gulped, unable to look at Trent '—about the man who wanted your land, without anyone knowing I was Harry Shaw's daughter. I thought people would speak more freely if they didn't know who I was.

'Why didn't you tell *me* you were going away, Harry?' she said accusingly. 'Where have you *been*?'

Harry reached out to squeeze her hand. 'First things first, love. Where have *you* been staying? Here in my house? Is that why that flywire screen's been tampered with? You had to climb in a window, did you? I must give you a key.'

'Sandra has been staying with me,' Trent answered for her. 'We met by accident. Literally,' he said, with a brief twitch of his lip. He explained in a few brief words. Harry, Sandra noticed, didn't seem as dismayed as she would have expected at the revelation that she had been a guest of Trent Corbin's for the past few days. In fact, he looked decidedly self-satisfied, like a cat about to lick out a bowl of cream!

'Well, Harry, I guess you'll want some time alone with your daughter,' Trent said. His expression was closed, his eyelids lowered, veiling his eyes, giving no clue to what he was thinking. 'Why don't you both join me for a late lunch—say in half an hour? I imagine you won't have much food in your house, Harry, until you go shopping?'

'Sit down to a meal with *you*, Corbin? No, thanks,' Harry said ungraciously. 'I don't think we're on civil enough terms for polite chit-chat. You'll feel even less like it when you hear what I have to tell you,' he said, with a faint smirk.

Trent's eyes pierced his for a long moment. 'You've hired some professional demonstrators, Harry, is that it?' he drawled at length, his tone sardonic.

Harry gave a snort. 'I won't need to use demonstrators, Corbin. I have a far more reliable way of keeping your hands off my land.'

Trent's brows shot up. 'Try me, Harry,' he invited impassively. 'Better still...' the corner of his mouth curved '...keep your *coup de grâce* until after we've eaten, if you think it will spoil a good meal. Whatever it is, I'm sure that having your daughter at lunch with us will prevent us coming to blows.' He moved to the door. 'You'll both come?'

'Harry, please say yes,' Sandra urged, slipping an arm through her father's. 'We need to get this all sorted out.' She was afraid that if the two men parted ways now the chasm between them would widen even further, forging a wedge between Trent and herself just as they were starting to draw closer.

'It wouldn't feel right,' Harry said gruffly, 'breaking bread with a man who's trying to drive me out of my home...using threats and vandalism.' He glowered at Trent.

Trent frowned, halting at the door. 'I've never made threats to you, Harry. Or sent anyone else to make them for me. And if by "vandalism" you're talking about your vegetables——'

'Of course I'm talking about my vegetables!' Harry snapped. 'The threats...well, no, you're too smart to make them to my face. But your loyal sidekick Roland, who blindly carries out *your* orders, did. He told me that if I didn't agree to sell up I'd get hurt, or unfor-

tunate things would start to happen to my property. And right after that my vegetables were dug up.'

'So...' A dangerous flame kindled deep in Trent's grey eyes. 'Roland's lied to me for the last time!' His voice was ominously low, boding ill for Roland. 'He denied he'd had anything to do with the damage to your vegetables. He insisted he'd seen kids hanging around your place. The police put the damage down to them.

'I'll deal with it, Harry,' he grated. 'You won't need to worry about threats any more. Or damage to your property. Roland's leaving. He'll be gone before tonight. I can see I made a mistake in taking him on at all.'

'Trent, no!' Sandra cried, dismayed that he might also mean he regretted what he had done for Roland's wife, because of the way his kindness had rebounded on him. She was afraid that it would make him retreat behind that cold, uncaring wall again, preventing anyone from getting too close...preventing *her* from getting too close.

'Roland didn't do any real harm,' she pleaded in the blond giant's defence. 'Vegetables can easily be replanted. I think he's basically a simple, gentle man at heart, Trent...a man with so much love for his wife that he desperately wanted to repay the man who saved her.'

As she'd uttered the words 'with so much love for his wife' she'd caught a faint flicker in Trent's eyes—a fleeting softness?—but in the next instant it was gone, his face hardening to granite.

'I was a fool to expose myself to Roland's gratitude,' he grated. 'I broke a rule I've long lived by: never have personal contact with the people you do things for.' His mouth twisted. 'I won't make that mistake again.'

'But you will still do things for people,' Sandra murmured, almost to herself, a knowing light in her eyes. 'Because you're not the uncaring monster you like to make out you are.'

'Well, we'll soon know,' Harry put in with a rueful lift of his lip. He was eyeing his daughter oddly. 'When Corbin hears what I have to say after lunch, that will be the test.' He shot Trent a challenging look.

Trent nodded slowly. 'So we agree to be civilised and break bread together before you hit me with this revelation of yours, Harry?'

'Agreed. But you won't like what I have to tell you,' Harry warned.

'I'm already quaking in my shoes,' Trent said drily, and turned and left them.

'That's the first human thing I've ever heard him say,' was Harry's gruff comment.

'Oh, Harry. He's more human than you'll ever know.' Sandra shook her head at him, a pensive smile on her lips. 'You two men!' she despaired with a sigh. 'You might have called a truce. But how long before you'll be locked in battle again, I wonder?'

'Ah,' said Harry, his lips spreading in a smile, 'but the battle is already won, my love. You'll see.'

Trent's hand brushed down her arm as he helped Sandra into a chair at his dining-room table. She felt the fine hairs on her skin lifting in response, and wondered if he felt the same excitement at a mere touch from *her*. He had told her, not once but several times, that he wanted her. But did he still want her now that Harry had come back? Now that Harry had come back *gloating*? She still didn't know what her father had been up to in his absence. He was making her wait too.

'Sit here opposite your father, Sandra.' Trent's voice was like a caress, his breath warmly intimate on her cheek as he bent over her. He was showing no visible sign of any tension or annoyance at the little game Harry was playing. But then, Trent Corbin was a master at masking his feelings.

'I've invited Roland to join us,' he surprised them by announcing, adding before Harry could protest, 'He'll still be leaving this evening, as I told you. But before he goes he wants to apologise to you, Harry. Since we've agreed to be civilised over lunch...' a mocking note curled through his voice '...I was sure you'd have no objection.'

Harry shrugged. 'I've no objection. Let him stay to hear what I have to say,' he invited, a similarly mocking light glowing in his crinkled blue eyes.

There was an awkward moment when Roland lumbered in, head bowed, eyes downcast, but Harry graciously accepted the giant's mumbled apology, even accepting Roland's outstretched hand.

'I meant no harm to you personally, Mr Shaw,' Roland said gruffly. 'I thought you were holding out for more money and I was trying to hurry things along, knowing Mr Corbin *needs* your land before he can get his resort under way. I knew he'd already gone out of his way to offer you a——'

'No speeches, Roland,' Trent cut in. 'Just the apology will suffice. Ah, Magda.' He nodded to the housekeeper as she poked her head round the door. 'Yes, we're ready, thanks.'

It wasn't the most comfortable of meals, but nobody broke the uneasy truce by starting an argument or treading on delicate ground. Roland, who barely uttered a word throughout, seemed more resigned than resentful at the prospect of leaving.

He's accepted Trent's decision, Sandra thought, relieved to see him showing no sign of animosity towards either Trent or Harry. He's going to leave without any fuss or bitterness.

The atmosphere over lunch—in her mind at least—took on a strangely unreal, almost dream-like quality. Maybe it was simply reaction, a weight lifting from her now that Harry had turned up, safe and sound. She only knew that she was pricklingly conscious of Trent sitting

at the head of the table, an unusually benign, attentive host.

She hoped that her father was beginning to see Trent in a more generous light now, and to realise that his fears about Trent Corbin had been baseless. The threats and stand-over tactics had come from Roland, acting on his own, not from Trent.

She found her thoughts straying back to Trent, found herself wishing the meal were over, wishing she could be alone with him, wishing they could talk things over in private, or, better still, not talk at all...

'Well, now, Harry...' Trent's voice, subtly different now—challenging? Mocking? Wary?—intruded on her dreamy thoughts. 'You've been bursting to tell us something all through lunch.' He leaned back in his chair, his coffee cup poised in mid-air. 'The floor's all yours.'

Sandra glanced across the table at her father as he gave a self-satisfied grin. 'It's very simple. Tonight I'm driving down to Nowra to have dinner with someone from Sydney. The fellow's down this way looking over selected homes in the area... with a specific purpose in mind,' he added mysteriously.

'Tomorrow morning he's coming to Kaoga Bay to look at *my* house. With a view to...' his grin grew wider '...giving it a National Trust classification! My house is an authentic Victorian home, and once it's listed,' he announced triumphantly, 'nobody will be allowed to pull it down!'

Sandra drew in her breath, her eyes leaping to Trent's face. She expected to see shock...stunned dismay...fury. Or that cold chilling devil's gleam in his eyes.

Instead she saw him raise his brows—his only visible reaction. Then his lips parted slightly—not to rant and rave, but to mutter drily, 'Ah, so you've outfoxed me, Harry. Full marks.' In the same calm tone, with a faint barb this time, he added, 'So that's why you skipped off in such secrecy. Worried I might find out what you

were up to, were you, and take some drastic countermeasure?'

'Actually,' Harry admitted, his blue eyes meeting Trent's steadily, 'I had a quite different plan up my sleeve originally. I went to Sydney to investigate *you*.'

'Oh, yes?' Trent said softly. Sandra held her breath, aware of Roland tensing in his chair at the end of the table, like an adder preparing to strike.

'I'd already hired a private detective, you see,' Harry admitted blithely, 'and I was anxious to see what he'd come up with. I was hoping he'd dug up some dirt on you, Corbin, that was sufficiently damaging to discredit you, so that nobody would want to do any more business with you and you certainly wouldn't be able to build your resort at Kaoga Bay!'

'You *bastard*!' The roar came from Roland, his great fists thudding down on the table in front of him. 'You'll never find any dirt on Mr Corbin. Dig all you like!'

'Strangely, Roland,' Harry said coolly, 'you're right. I didn't. So I switched to plan B. The National Trust. Just as effective, wouldn't you say, Corbin?' His eyes clashed with Trent's. 'And less unpleasant, for all concerned. This way your reputation remains intact. And so does my house.'

'Harry, you're all heart.' Trent clapped his hands in mocking tribute, his face coolly impassive, his eyes hooded, hard to read.

Sandra scanned the hard lines and planes of his face, looking for a clue to his real thoughts. Was he angry? Bitterly disappointed? It was hard to tell.

Roland heaved himself to his feet. 'There's something I want to do before I go,' he said gruffly. He was looking at Harry. 'I want to fix the damage I did to your vegetable garden. And plant new vegetables. I'll drive to the nearest nursery now and buy them. Whatever you want.'

'Well...I don't know.' Harry frowned up at him, quick mistrust in his eyes.

'Please say yes, Harry,' Sandra begged. 'Can't you see that Roland's trying to make amends for what he did to your vegetables?'

'All right.' Harry gave in with a jerk of his shoulder. 'Thanks,' he said grudgingly. 'You'd better come back with me now, then, and I'll work out what vegetables I want you to put in.' He pushed back his chair and stood up.

'I'll get some tools and drive over straight away,' Roland said, and shambled out.

As the others rose to leave the table, Harry thrust out his hand to Trent. 'My apologies for misjudging you, Corbin,' he said in his gruff voice. 'No bad feelings?'

The corners of Trent's mouth curved upwards as he took the proffered hand. 'If I'd known you felt so strongly about staying put, Harry, I might have gone about things differently. But I had to make sure you weren't just holding out for a better deal,' he said with a touch of his old cynicism. 'Plenty do play that game.'

Then he made an admission, surprising both father and daughter. 'I fear I have a far too jaded view of life and people. Your daughter——' he glanced at Sandra '—has pointed out my shortcomings on numerous occasions. I'm trying my best to mend my ways.'

She gave him a smile as she met his eyes, a smile from her heart, warm and light. 'You see, Harry?' she said, though she was incapable of plucking her gaze away from Trent's. 'I told you he was human.'

'He shows promise.' Harry wasn't admitting it *yet*.

'Harry, you're a hard man.' Trent only then broke eye contact with Sandra. 'I'd rather have you on my side than against me.'

'Likewise,' Harry muttered. But he gave a crooked smile as he said it. He glanced at Sandra, his face turning

bland. 'Are you coming to stay at my place, love, or staying on here till you go back to town?'

She hesitated, feeling helplessly torn.

'She'd better stay here for tonight, Harry,' Trent put in smoothly, 'since you say you'll be driving down to Nowra this evening, and having your friend from the Trust going over your house tomorrow. You won't want to get caught up in all that, will you, Sandra?' His eyes caught and held hers.

She felt herself melting under his gaze, mesmerised by what she saw in the grey depths, her pulse skittering.

'No...not really,' she said, a faint tremor in her voice. When she saw a tiny flame flicker in Trent's eyes she felt sure that her knees would buckle beneath her and her heart would leap from her chest.

'Well, you'll know where she is, Harry.' Trent was still looking at *her* as he said it. 'Join us for lunch again tomorrow, why don't you, after your visitor from the Trust has gone?' He flicked his gaze away from Sandra's at last, to give Harry a wry smile. 'You can give us a report on the big inspection.'

'Whichever way it goes?' Harry raised an eyebrow.

'Whichever way it goes.'

'Well, thanks... I just might do that,' said Harry. He stepped over to give his daughter a peck on the cheek. 'See you later, love. Be good.'

She flushed as she caught the speculative gleam in her father's eyes. 'No more vanishing acts, Harry,' she admonished in return, hoping—but not caring too much—that he would put her flushed cheeks down to the wine at lunch. 'OK?' She flashed him a smile.

'Deal,' said Harry. As he headed for the door he had a last word for Trent—astonishing them both. 'If my daughter had to be run over by anybody,' he said gruffly, 'I think maybe she picked the right guy.' Then he ducked through the door out of sight.

'I have a feeling I've just had the ultimate accolade,' Trent said, looking down at Sandra, his gaze, half bemused, half tender, swallowing hers.

She gulped, suddenly feeling shy and more than a little vulnerable, now that she was alone with him at last. The way he was looking at her...

'Harry's not the only one who misjudged you, Trent,' she said huskily. 'I've been so wrong about you—accusing you of hounding Harry to his death, thinking the worst of you, thinking you were a—a black-hearted devil who didn't care about anybody or anything...other than snapping up properties and making money.'

'You weren't wrong about me,' he said heavily. A quiver ran through her as he curled his hands over her shoulders and pulled her close. 'I *didn't* care about anybody or anything. Or care what people thought of me.' His eyes speared hers. 'Until I met you.'

Her eyelids flickered under his gaze. What was he saying? That he *felt* something for her? He'd never made any secret of the fact that he *wanted* her. Was it possible that his desire for her was already growing into something deeper, stronger, more meaningful...that he was starting to care for her the way she had come to care—it was no use denying it—for him? Or was that wishful thinking?

A cool shadow flitted across her face. It was like a breath of caution. Could a man whose heart was dead ever learn to feel again, care again, *love* again? Would Trent ever be able to turn his back on the trauma and guilt of the past? He'd told her once that he had nothing left to give. So what precisely did he want from her? A momentary escape from his torment? Forgetfulness? Was that all?

'Trent, I——'

She broke off as Magda came back into the room to clear the table. Trent dropped his hands from her

shoulders and caught her hand, tugging her across the room to the door.

She felt a flutter of panic. 'Trent, maybe I ought to go after Harry after all...to be with him while Roland is there. To—to keep an eye on them,' she faltered, knowing it was just an excuse, just a means to gain some breathing space.

Things were moving too quickly, far too quickly. After the shocks and revelations of the past few hours the two of them were in just the mood to say and do anything, *promise* anything. She might agree to something she would regret later, and end up badly hurt. Already a mere touch, a mere look from Trent was enough to send sanity flying out the window.

Trent waved her through the doorway and into the passage. 'I think now that Roland's seen the error of his ways,' he said unworriedly, 'all he wants to do is make amends.' He paused, lifting her hand to his lips and kissing the tip of each finger, so exquisitely slowly and sensuously that she was sure he must feel the tingles that ran from her fingers all the way down to her toes, sure he must hear the erratic thud of her heartbeat.

She gulped, wildly seeking a diversion—any diversion. 'Trent, what will you do now that Harry—now that you——?' she found herself floundering.

'Now that Harry has found a way to stop me buying his property?' he assisted her, his expression bland.

She nodded, catching her breath as his lips found another fingertip. But this time, instead of kissing it, he drew the pink tip into his mouth and sucked slowly, in a way that was as erotic as it was tender.

'Trent, d-don't!' she gasped. 'I can't think!'

He gave a soft laugh. 'Do you need to think?'

'Yes!' she croaked. 'I—I want to know what you intend to do. I mean——' she flushed hotly '—about your resort. What will you d-do about it now?' she babbled, groaning inwardly as she heard the way she

was stammering. What was she afraid of? Or *most* afraid of? Him . . . or herself?

'Mmm . . . well, I'll have to think about that.' But not now, he seemed to be saying as his lips moved to the next finger and sucked the tip of that one too. Then he blew gently on the moist tip, before curling his tongue round it in the most titillating way.

'I—I really think we should go and help Harry!' she gasped, snatching back her hand.

His mouth quirked. 'You won't escape so easily to-night, Sandra,' he vowed, his eyes showing more amusement than chagrin, as if he knew it would only be a matter of time before she gave in. 'Very well, we'll go over to Harry's. There's something I want to do there anyway—mend the flywire screen I damaged getting into his house. You can come and watch.'

'I'm not completely helpless!' she snapped, her nerves at fever pitch. She didn't *want* to escape, that was the truth of it.

His lips eased further. 'No, you're not. Far from it. Sandra . . .' His tone changed, his face serious now. 'There's something I want you to know.'

'Y-yes?'

His hand closed over the fingers he had been teasing with his lips a moment ago. 'I might not care what other people think of me,' he said, 'but I do care what you think of me, Sandra.' The silver eyes impaled hers. 'That paternity suit . . .'

Her heart jumped. 'Trent, there's no——'

'The child wasn't mine,' he cut in. 'I'm not denying I slept with the woman—just once.' His mouth twisted. 'One night was all she needed. Unknown to me, she was already pregnant . . . and she knew it.'

'She . . . admitted it?'

'Later, yes. After her ex-boyfriend read about the case in the papers and claimed the child was his. She caved in then and owned up, retracting publicly—though that,

of course,' he said drily, 'didn't attract the publicity that her original *false* claim did. I believe,' he added with an ironic half-smile, 'the two of them are married now.'

'How could she?' Sandra cried, her eyes throwing out sparks of indignation. 'What made her do such a thing to you? The prospect of money?'

'Who knows? That, and revenge, perhaps—wanting to hit back at her man because he'd walked out on her—presumably before she knew she was pregnant.'

'It's a wonder you didn't sue *her*—for slander!' she burst out. She tilted her head at him, her eyes narrowing. 'But of course you wouldn't, would you? You wouldn't have cared what people thought of you.'

'Not then, no.' A silvery flame flickered in his eyes. 'But maybe I would now. If you...' He drew in his breath, swallowing the rest. Deep in his eyes gleamed emotions that she hardly dared try to read. 'I haven't wanted or trusted another woman since. Until now. Until I met you.'

A choking lump rose in her throat. She gulped it away, her eyes darkening in pain. 'How—how can you trust me,' she whispered, 'after I came into your home under false pretences? After I admitted I was hoping to hurt you? After hiding so much from you?'

The eyes holding hers seemed to soften. 'You had good reason. It was understandable.' His lips curved in a slow smile. 'You're not much of a liar anyway. It's obvious you don't make a habit of it, of hiding things from people. I always knew—sensed—when you weren't being open with me...when you were holding something back.'

She stared at him. 'You—you did?' She flushed guiltily. 'I see now why you kept such a close eye on me.'

'Oh, that wasn't the only reason I kept a close eye on you.' His voice was caressingly soft, and she felt light-

headed at the glinting warmth in his eyes. 'But we'll pursue that later.' He stepped reluctantly away from her. 'Let's get over to Harry's,' he said roughly, 'and hope the afternoon passes quickly, hmm?'

CHAPTER ELEVEN

THE rest of the afternoon passed in a torment of exquisite suspense. Sandra felt giddy with anticipation, hardly noticing what was going on around her. She was vaguely aware of Rōland crouched over the tumbled soil of Harry's vegetable patch, planting the vegetables Harry had chosen . . . of Harry rushing to and fro between the house and the yard, getting the place shipshape for the inspection the next day . . . of her own hands obediently passing a nail or a tool to Trent as they repaired the flywire screen together and helped Harry with other jobs that needed doing.

She felt a certain bemusement that Trent Corbin, so long her father's arch-enemy, so long the black-hearted villain of the piece, was now going out of his way to help Harry save the very house he had so badly wanted to demolish for his own use.

Was it guilt that was driving him? Guilt over what Roland—*his* right-hand man—had done to Harry? Did he blame himself, since it was his own ruthless pursuit of Harry's property that had led Roland—anxious to pay back his debt to Trent—to resort to threats and vandalism to hasten things along?

Or, she wondered hopefully, was it simply that Trent *wanted* to help Harry, because he had grown to care about both father and daughter, to see their point of view?

There had always been a spark of humanity in Trent, she mused, much as he had tried to hide it, and deny it. Hadn't he helped to save the life of Roland's sick wife? Hadn't he given Roland a job when the blond giant was

down and out? Didn't he build homes for the old and sick, and give liberally, without publicising it, to needy charities?

But she didn't dwell for too long on Trent's motives. Other thoughts kept intruding, heart-quivering thoughts of what lay ahead later this evening, thoughts that brought an ache of anticipation to her throat and a curl of warmth deep down inside her.

Roland was still labouring in the garden when Harry vanished inside to change for his dinner down the coast.

'We'll be off too,' Trent shouted after him, and Sandra's heart did a slow somersault. 'Will you be having dinner with us, Roland, before you go?' he called out to the giant, and Sandra wondered if he was about to relent and allow Roland to stay on.

But Trent's face was closed and cold. There was no sign of relenting there.

Roland glanced up and shook his head, not looking either of them in the eye. 'No, thanks, Mr Corbin. I'll finish up here and then I'll be off. I want to look for another job before my wife gets back home.' Surprisingly, there was no self-pity in his voice. He sounded matter-of-fact and respectful. Even grateful.

Sandra felt a flare of sympathy at the thought of his wife, still recuperating from her operation. 'Where will you live, Roland?' she asked. 'What will you do?'

He shrugged, sliding a look up at her. 'I'll find something. Another caretaker job, maybe, or a labouring job. Where doesn't matter. My wife can stay with her sister until I find a place to live.'

He had savings, Sandra remembered. Just as well, she reflected, doubting that Trent would have given the giant any severance pay after what he had done. Unless, for his wife's sake...

'Goodbye, Roland,' Trent said, with no softening in his voice.

'I won't forget what you did for me, Mr Corbin,' were Roland's parting words, drifting after them as Trent steered Sandra away. There was no malice in the giant's tone. Nothing of the sort.

No, she thought, looking up at Trent with a faint mistiness in her eyes. I bet you won't be letting him go away empty-handed. You like to make out you're so hard and unfeeling, but you're not, underneath. There's a lot of goodness in you, Trent Corbin, and I'm seeing more of it each hour, each minute, each second, as the cold, unfeeling layers peel away.

Could *she* possibly have had anything to do with the change in him?

His gaze collided with hers and the look in his eyes set her nerves fluttering again, sending tremors rippling through her.

She wasn't sure how she got through their light evening meal of chicken pie and salad without screaming for a break in the tension. There were only the two of them at the table, Magda having left their dinner for them and retired early to watch a special programme on TV.

All Sandra's senses were vividly alive, on edge, as she and Trent sat facing each other across the table. The pale grey shirt he'd changed into before dinner was made of a fabric so thin and soft that it made her want to reach out and run her fingers over its silky smoothness and feel the muscles she glimpsed underneath.

Tonight she had discarded her jeans for a flared black skirt—another of Trent's sister's cast-offs. With it she wore a blouse of her own, its soft powdery blue a colour which she knew intensified the blue of her eyes.

She picked at her food, hardly noticing what she ate. All her senses, all her thoughts were focused on Trent. Even their conversation, light and varied though it was, had an unreal, almost ethereal quality about it—just words that neither one was really paying attention to because they were both too intent on each other.

When Trent finally pulled back her chair and held out his hand to her she knew, with a surge of exhilaration, that she had been waiting all evening, all day, all week—maybe all her life!—for this moment.

'Come up to the tower with me, Sandra...' His voice was huskily inviting. 'Nobody will interrupt us there.' A tiny flame burned in his eyes, trapping her own like a powerful magnet.

Her heartbeat accelerated. She knew what she would be agreeing to if she said yes, but the needs of her body seemed to be ruling her head, and all she could do was nod, flicking her tongue over suddenly dry lips.

He took her hand and led her from the room. 'We'll put on some music... take our time getting more...' he paused '... intimately acquainted.' His eyes held hers in a seductive challenge.

She shivered in anticipation even as a spark of sanity glowed briefly. This was madness, sheer madness! She knew what he wanted from her... not love, not commitment. All he felt for her was lust, passion, a physical need. All he wanted from her was a few hours of forgetfulness... or maybe a few days, a few weeks if she was lucky.

He would be a wonderful lover, she had no doubt, but she would never be able to reach him. He would never offer her his heart, his love. His heart was dead. He'd said so. If she wanted love, or commitment, or anything lasting, she would never get it from Trent Corbin. She had better have no illusions about that. She *had* no illusions.

And at this moment she didn't care, making no protest as he led her up the stairs, her heightened senses making her vividly aware of the shiny smoothness of the cedar hand-rail, of the pattern on each carpeted stair, even of a tiny flaw in the wallpaper, her ears picking up each squeak of the old wooden stairs, her nostrils flaring at the faint musty scent of old timber and carpet.

But most of all she was aware of Trent Corbin, the man, as he almost hauled her up the stairs, the palm of his enveloping hand warm on her skin, his muscular thigh brushing against hers, their breath mingling.

Only when they were in the moon-drenched tower did he release her, just long enough to slip a compact disc into his player, again not bothering to switch on the lamp beside it. She tried to keep her eyes from straying to the large couch along one wall, turning her gaze out to sea, trying to keep her mind from flooding with the image of him holding her, kissing her, touching her all over.

As the romantic strains of a soaring violin teased her senses almost to screaming-point, Trent slid his hands over her shoulders and swung her round to face him, sending an involuntary tremor through her.

'I've been waiting all day for this.' His voice had thickened, and his eyes under the heavy brows were like piercing silver slits, trapping hers.

She couldn't move, couldn't breathe.

'Come here . . . close to me.'

She caught her breath as his arm curled round her waist, dragging her hard up against him, moulding the firm muscles of his chest to the fullness of her breasts, the erratic beat of his heart echoing like a wild jungle drum through her body.

'You feel so good,' he said hoarsely, moving his lips over the shining mass of her hair, then grazing them across her forehead, over her eyelids, down her cheeks, imprinting hot kisses on her skin. 'More than good.'

It did feel good. *He* felt good. Never before had a man felt so *right*. She leaned against him, trembling and breathless, intoxicated by the tension she could feel in him, her body quivering in anticipation of what was going to happen next.

'Don't run away from me this time, Sandra.' His voice was low and gravelly, raising goose-bumps on her skin. 'I've been wanting this . . . wanting *you* . . . from the

moment you first looked up at me with those haunting, incredibly blue eyes of yours.'

Her lashes fluttered upwards. 'You mean——'

'I mean on that first day, yes...when I found you lying by the roadside.' His fingers curved under her chin, tilting her face up. 'When I took off your helmet and your golden hair tumbled down over my fingers. You looked up at me, and I felt something I hadn't felt since my...' He flicked his tongue over his lips, letting the words drift away.

'You still can't say her name, Trent?' she whispered, the small hope that had flared for an instant fading just as quickly. 'You won't ever come to terms with what happened,' she said with a wistful sigh, 'until you can face up to it...talk about it...about *her*. And your son. Until you can let go of the pain.'

She felt him tense, his eyes gleaming into hers, and thought for a second that he was going to ignore her plea and fling the past to oblivion with a savage kiss. But instead he let a ragged sigh whisper from his lips and said, in a voice that was raw and strained, but steady, 'Maybe you're right. You usually are.

'I think you would have liked Celia, Sandra. She cared about people, and they seemed to sense it, respond to it. Everyone loved her. She was very genuine...natural. No airs or pretences. She was so different from other women I'd known...'

Her eyes encouraged him to go on, even though it was painful to hear him talk of his love for another woman, and even though her body was aching for other, more selfish intimacies. But she knew that she would never have any hope of winning his heart and soul, as well as his body, until the demons haunting him were faced and excised.

'She adored children. She was ecstatic when she fell pregnant a few months after we married.' Trent frowned. He was looking past her now, looking back to that

painful time. 'In the spring after our son was born I took them both to the mountains for a holiday. Celia was feeling a bit down. Postnatal blues, her doctor called it.

'The break away from home did seem to help. I used to get up each morning and light the wood fire to heat up the cottage while she and the baby were still sleeping. Our son, Tristan, was just…nine months old.' The words seemed dragged from him. 'Celia and I only had two years together. Two happy, perfect years that I wiped out in one moment of thoughtless, reckless stupidity!'

'No, Trent!' Sandra stirred in his arms. 'You haven't lost those two happy years; you'll always have them. Only *you* can take them away.' Gently, chidingly, she added, 'You've been so busy feeling guilty about that fire, Trent, and turning yourself into a cold-hearted automaton to blot out the pain, that you've blotted out everything else as well—the happy memories along with the painful ones. Trent, you'll never stop hurting until you——'

He silenced her with a finger to her lips. 'I feel no pain when I'm with you,' he muttered thickly, nuzzling his lips into the smooth hollow of her throat.

She sighed even as an instant flame leapt inside her. She wanted nothing more than to forget the past too, but she sensed a need in him that was even greater than the aching need of their bodies, and somehow she dragged up the strength to make one last appeal to him.

'Don't lose those good times you had, Trent—the happiness, the love you shared with your family.' She paused, adding softly, 'You will if you keep denying the past, pretending it didn't exist. Some people can have more loving and happiness in two years than a lot of couples have in a lifetime.'

Sensing that she was getting through to him at last, she pleaded, 'Cherish the time you had together, Trent. You owe it to Celia and Tristan.'

He didn't speak for a long moment, his face still buried in the curve of her throat. When she felt a muscle twitch at his jaw, a lump filled her throat and she knew instinctively that the reason for his silence was that he didn't trust himself to speak.

'I do love to hear violins,' she murmured, bringing her hand up to stroke his rough cheek, wanting to show him that she understood. 'I always wanted to learn to play the violin, you know.'

As the exquisite sounds soared and curled around them, she could feel the tension flowing out of him. He raised his head, his eyes seeking hers, and she saw only tenderness, not the pain she had been expecting, in the grey depths. 'Why didn't you?' he asked huskily.

'My stepfather didn't like the idea. Practising a violin at home can be rather hard on the nerves.' In the wash of the moonlight their eyes locked and swam together, and she was barely conscious of what she was saying. 'I learned to play the piano instead.'

'There's a lot I'd like to know about you.' Trent's lips brushed over hers. 'But right now all I can think of is how much I want you... need you.' His lips circled her mouth, his tongue sliding over its softness. 'And how much I've wanted you since that very first day.'

She gulped. 'You didn't show it. If I recall,' she teased, though she was finding it hard to think at all, let alone speak, with his mouth so temptingly close, 'you berated me... soundly.'

'It was the most effective way of blocking out the way I felt,' he said, his words muffled against her lips. 'I thought I'd succeeded tolerably well...but I was fooling myself. I still wanted you, ached for you. I tried to rationalise it, make it into something unimportant, insignificant: you intrigued me...you challenged me...you diverted me.

'The truth is,' he growled, a feverish glitter in his eyes, 'you were already in my blood, Sandra, pounding

through my veins. I can't do without you. Don't run away from me now!'

Her lips parted, a deep tremor shaking through her body. 'I won't run away, Trent,' she promised, and knew as she said it that the die was cast, that there was no turning back now. And at this moment she didn't care that he only wanted her for the need he felt now, and only to find forgetfulness in her arms. He wanted her, and she wanted him, and his need for her right now was greater than her need for something deeper and more lasting, overriding even the thought of the pain and hurt that she would undoubtedly suffer later on.

She curled her arm round his neck and arched her back, feeling her breasts swell, their tips tingling to hardness as she pressed them into the cushioning warmth of his chest. A low, guttural sound broke from his throat as his mouth opened over hers and captured it hungrily, his fingers tangling in the silky waves of her hair.

She felt mindless under his kisses, aware only of the glorious sensations bursting through her, fanning the flames inside her, driving her wild with the need for even greater intimacy.

Trent wrenched his mouth from hers, just long enough to rasp, 'I want you...so much!' His hand was fumbling with her blouse, tugging it out of the waistband of her skirt, sliding his fingers up underneath. They paused at her lacy bra, brushing over the throbbing mound of her breast with teasing slowness, irresistibly drawn to the bare swell of her cleavage above. Her breasts heaved in aching invitation, her heart thudding out of control under his seeking fingers.

A soft moan was dragged from deep in her throat as his hand slipped inside her bra and began to squeeze the soft flesh underneath.

'I want you, Sandra...all of you!' he said thickly, and she uttered no protest as he started to drag her towards the couch.

He didn't lower her down straight away, instead unbuttoning her blouse with exquisitely painful slowness, peeling it back over her shoulders, and letting it fall in rippling folds to the floor. Already his fingers were fumbling with the clasp of her bra, loosening it, then discarding it as he had her blouse.

He gazed down at her. 'You're a vision,' he whispered almost reverently, and bent his head to kiss the smooth fullness of first one breast, then the other. Then he drew back his head and brought both hands up to cover her breasts, pressing his palms into the soft flesh with gentle, erotic pressure, feeling the taut peaks harden further under his teasing.

She gave a muffled groan of dismay as he paused; she felt his body stiffen, felt his hands slide from her breasts, a sudden icy fear quenching the fires inside her as she saw that he was looking past her, staring at the window, glazed shock in his eyes—or disbelief, perhaps, as if he were seeing . . .

'Trent, what is it?' she whispered fearfully. Was he seeing an image of his dead wife Celia? Was he realising that he would never escape from her, or from his past, and that no woman, not even a woman he believed was in his blood, pounding through his veins, whom he'd called a vision only a moment ago, could blot out the memories and the guilt that still tormented him?

His mouth slashed open. He let out a ragged yelp. 'Harry's house! Oh, my God, it's on fire!'

She was too shocked to react for a second. Then she gave a choked cry, her head whipping round, her eyes widening in horror as she saw the flickering glow coming from the darkness of Harry's house. Trent was already tearing himself away from her, leaping for the stairs.

'Call the fire department!' he rasped over his shoulder. 'The number's by the phone in the hall!'

'Trent!' she shrieked, coming to life and snatching up her blouse before flying after him. 'Wait! Harry's not

in danger—he's not at home, remember! Wh-what are you going to do?'

'Make sure!' he ripped back.

'Trent, no! B-be careful!'

By the time she reached the phone in the hall the front door had long since slammed shut. She found the emergency numbers and within seconds had put through the call and had an assurance that help was on the way.

As she bounded across the hall, buttoning her blouse as she ran, Magda burst from one of the rooms.

'What's going on? First Mr Corbin storms out of the house, now you!'

Sandra blurted out what had happened as she lunged for the door, not looking to see if Magda was following as she bolted out into the night and across the moonlit yard, dodging through the gum trees and scrub dividing the two properties. As she neared Harry's cottage, the sound of exploding glass brought a sharp gasp to her lips, her eyes dilating in horror as she saw orange flames leaping from Harry's front windows.

'Trent!' she croaked, knowing there wouldn't be four men to hold him back this time if he plunged into the fire looking for Harry. She had no fears for her father. She was sure he wouldn't be back yet from his dinner in Nowra. But she did have very real fears for Trent.

By the time she reached the cottage, the entire front section was ablaze, flames even licking from the roof. She could hear the roar of the fire inside, and other sounds she couldn't account for, sounds that heightened her fears. There was no hope of getting into the house the front way, so she charged round the back, dragging in a relieved breath as she glanced across at the garage and saw the deep, moonlit cavity inside. Harry's car wasn't at home—which meant that Harry wasn't either!

Concerned solely for Trent's safety now—Harry's house at this moment was a minor consideration—she stumbled in through the open back door, into a wall of

thick smoke, almost tripping over a garden hose running in from outside. She could hear hissing, spitting sounds as water sprayed on to the flames. As the smoke filled her nostrils and choked up her throat, she started to cough, and clapped a hand over her nose and mouth.

Then she saw Trent, half crouched in the passage, with one arm raised to protect his face from the heat and flames, his other hand gripping the hose, pointing it into the fire, trying to keep the roaring flames from spreading from the front rooms to the rear of the house.

She heard a blood-chilling creaking sound and screamed a warning a split-second before the timbers supporting the living-room ceiling collapsed, throwing a whoosh of flames, smoke and glowing sparks at Trent. He flinched, but resisted stepping back.

'Trent, your hair's on fire! Get back!' she screeched, and hurled herself at him, beating at his hair with her hands.

'Sandra!' Ignoring her flailing arms, he threw an arm round her waist and bore her back across the room and out of the house, the gushing hose still in his hand. 'You stay out here, you understand?' he bellowed, giving her a shove that sent her sprawling on to the brick paving. Then he ran back inside the house.

'Trent, *no!*' she screamed as she scrambled to her feet. 'You've done enough!' She almost sobbed in relief as a siren split the night air and a fire truck roared into the yard. Men in helmets and thick fire suits leapt from all directions, dragging hoses and yelling at her to stand back, and forcing Trent and his garden hose from the house.

Within seconds the powerful hoses were gushing water on to the fire, and a miraculously short time later the roaring flames began to subside. One of the firemen shouted out to them that the rear section of the house and the staircase and attic above had escaped the ravages of the fire and had suffered only smoke damage.

Thanks to Trent, Sandra thought, grasping his arm tightly. As she felt the tension in his muscles, she glanced up at him and gulped at what she saw in his face, in his eyes, sensing instinctively that he needed her comfort right now more than her gratitude.

'It's all right, Trent,' she whispered 'It's going to be all right.'

He looked down at her with glazed eyes. 'I couldn't save the front rooms of the house,' he said, his voice bleak. 'I tried...' He shook his head. 'There was nothing I could do.'

Her hand flew up to touch his cheek, his anguish piercing her heart. She'd sensed, as he'd groaned the words 'There was nothing I could do', that he wasn't thinking only of Harry's house. He was thinking of another house, another fire, the greatest tragedy of his life. He's reliving his worst nightmare, she thought, wishing she could wipe away his pain.

'Trent, nobody could have done more than you did. You saved my father's house; it's only the front rooms that have been destroyed, and without you the rest would have gone up too. You put your life at risk, Trent, at terrible risk...even knowing Harry wasn't inside. I...' She gulped, and faltered. 'Trent, I couldn't bear it if anything happened to you!' The words burst out. She couldn't hold them back.

She saw something flash in his eyes, the bright moonlight casting light and shadow across his face. 'You think I could bear it if anything happened to *you*?' The words seemed to be drawn from deep down in his throat, more a groan than a growl. 'All the time I was fighting the fire,' he said hoarsely, 'I was thinking of *you*, Sandra, thinking that *you* could have been in there if you'd decided to stay the night at Harry's. And when you plunged in behind me... I've never felt such fear!'

She knew instinctively that the fear he had felt had been for her, not for himself. 'It was like...it was like

history repeating itself! As if I'm fated in some ghastly
way. As if I'll always have the nightmare of knowing I
could lose any woman I come to care for!'

Even as the words 'any woman I come to care for'
shook through her, she was shaken even more by the
fact that he was stripping back his innermost emotions
and laying them raw before her, all the feelings and fears
he'd savagely blotted out, coldly denied, since the death
of his wife and child.

She reached up and caught his face between her hands.
'But history didn't repeat itself, Trent,' she said steadily.
'And you're not going to lose me... *I* was more in danger
of losing *you*,' she reminded him, her eyes burningly
tender. 'You put yourself in mortal danger tonight, Trent,
just as you did back then. If people hadn't stopped you
plunging into that inferno you would have died with your
wife and child!'

'For a long time I wished I *had* died with them.' His
voice was rough, still raw, but the eyes that met hers
were calmer now, accepting, a lot of the anguish gone.
'But now...hopefully——' she saw a new, softer light
smoulder to life in his eyes '—there's a reason for me
to go on living. A powerful reason.'

She felt a jolt rock through her. As their eyes locked
in mutual understanding, mingled with other, more
dizzying emotions, several things happened at once. A
police car swung into the yard, Harry's old car roared
in behind, and one of the firemen shouted that the fire
was out and they were now mopping up. While she and
Trent were filling Harry and the police in on what had
happened, Magda's plump figure emerged from the
gloom waving a white envelope at Trent.

'I found this,' she gasped out, still puffing from the
exertion of running. 'I thought it might be important.
It's from Roland. I'd know his untidy scrawl anywhere.'

Sandra saw a gleam leap to Trent's eyes as, tight-
lipped, he snatched the envelope from the housekeeper

and moved closer to the floodlight over Harry's garage to read it. 'I have a bad feeling about this,' he grated. Under the curious eyes of the two police officers, he ripped it open and tore out the note inside.

Sandra watched his face darken as he read it, saw his fists clench as he thrust it at her with a savage snarl. 'If I ever find him I'll kill him for this! Read it. Read it aloud!'

Her fingers trembled as she took the note from him, a gasp of dismay leaving her lips as she ran her eyes over the contents. With a glance at Harry, she shakily began to read:

'I never thought I could repay the debt I owe you, Mr Corbin, but now I have and we're square. Harry's got no choice but to sell to you now. A million thanks for all you've done for me and my wife. I'm not going to risk being sent to jail for this so I'll be heading off interstate to find a job. My wife can stay with her sister till I send for her. Good luck with the resort. R.'

Harry exploded. 'The *mongrel*! *He* set fire to my house! So that I'd have to sell my land to *you*.' He faced Trent accusingly. 'That bloody resort. You're to blame for this, Corbin!'

Sandra gave a pained cry. 'Harry! Stop that! Trent risked his life to *save* your house. It would be lying in ruins but for him. You owe him your *thanks*!'

Trent's harsh voice intervened. 'No, Harry's right. The blame does lie with me. It was my ruthless drive to own this entire headland and do what I liked with it that led to this. You'd better give the note to the sergeant, Sandra. It's evidence.'

She handed it over, her eyes still lashing her father. She was furious with Harry for his attack on Trent. And Trent was saying nothing in his own defence. Nothing! Just as he'd said nothing all those years ago after he'd failed to save his wife and child from another, more tragic

fire. He'd blamed himself then and he was blaming himself now, as if he felt he deserved the scorn and condemnation that people heaped on him. *Relished* it, even.

Taking a step towards Harry, she blazed, 'Trent could have been *killed* in that fire. Don't you realise what he's done for you? And he——'

'Leave it!' Trent's voice sliced over her. 'I could have prevented this happening, and we all know it. If I'd kicked Roland out the second I knew he was responsible for vandalising Harry's garden, instead of letting him hang around replanting vegetables and thinking up ways to set fire to the place, Harry's house would never have been in danger. *I* gave Roland the opportunity *and* the motivation in the first place. The blame lies fairly and squarely at my door!'

'No!' Sandra stamped her foot, her eyes flashing sapphire sparks. 'You're not going to blame yourself, Trent—not this time! We all know—and Roland knows it too, or he wouldn't be skipping off interstate—that you would never, *ever* condone a thing like this, no matter how badly you wanted Harry's land. If you did, why in the world would you have risked your life to save the one house that's standing in your way?'

Harry cleared his throat. 'My daughter's right,' he said gruffly, thrusting out his hand to Trent. 'I was way out of line blaming you. I should be *thanking* you. I do thank you. If the house is beyond repair, the land is yours. I won't stand in your way. There are other houses, other beaches, other rocks for fishing.'

Trent appeared to flinch. 'You think I'd take it from you now, or even *want* it, after this? You don't want to leave here, Harry. You've gone to enough lengths to convince me how much you want to stay put. And since it was my greed that led to all this it's my responsibility to do something about it. I'll rebuild your house for you, Harry. And restore it.'

Harry, instead of jumping at the offer, frowned. 'I can do without your pity, Corbin. You just want to appease your conscience. And once you've done that you'll go ahead and build your resort *around* my land, making things so darned uncomfortable for me, with tourists swarming all over the headland, that I'll end up *shoving* my land at you, *begging* you to take it!'

Trent actually threw back his head and laughed. 'I assure you, Harry, I won't be begging for your land. Nor will I be building a resort here after all. It's not feasible without your land.'

As Sandra's lips parted, Harry growled into the pause that followed, 'So you're going to be a martyr now.'

Trent shook his head. 'I'm no martyr, Harry. But maybe I have changed...in these past few days.' His eyes sought Sandra's, and she flushed as she met his gaze and saw what lay in the silver-grey depths, a deep, delicious shiver rippling through her. 'Your daughter, Harry, has had a lot to do with that—pointing out the error of my ways.'

Harry grinned suddenly. 'A chip off the old block,' he muttered with satisfaction.

Trent's lips spread in an answering grin. 'There was a time, Harry, when I believed that this property here was beyond you. I see now that nothing is beyond Harry Shaw.'

'Excuse me, sir.' One of the firemen stepped up from behind. 'We thought you'd like to know. We found a bar heater overturned in the house. That's how the fire started.'

'So that's how he did it, the bastard,' Harry growled.

'Er...just who is the man who wrote this note?' the police sergeant put in, brandishing Roland's note.

'Let me fill you in, Sergeant,' Trent said obligingly. But his face was grim.

CHAPTER TWELVE

IT WAS very late—the early hours of the morning, in fact—before Sandra found herself finally alone with Trent, Harry having retired to one of the spare bedrooms after accepting Trent's invitation to stay overnight.

'Don't go to bed just yet.'

Her heart quickened as Trent held out his hand to her and led her over to the sofa. The glowing embers of the log fire warmed them as he pulled her into the enticing curve of his shoulder.

She smiled up at him. 'What you did for Harry tonight,' she breathed huskily, 'meant the world to him, Trent, despite the way he carried on.'

He brushed some fine strands of hair from her face. She could feel his heartbeat, as unsteady as her own. 'Maybe I didn't do it for Harry,' he said. 'Maybe I did it for you.'

She felt a joyful leap inside her, only to squash her elation to gently chide him. 'I'd like to think you did it for Harry. For a man who was prepared to fight you . . . and win.'

His mouth curved into a smile—a smile that gladdened her heart. 'I've always admired a good fighter. And your father is certainly that. A bit like his daughter. Indomitable. Full of spirit. I knew from the beginning that you were going to be one hell of a challenge.'

Her eyes fluttered uncertainly under his. Was that all she had been to him? A challenge? What followed a challenge, after it was won? The victory feast, to be mutually enjoyed to the hilt? And then what? Thanks, and

goodbye? She felt something sink inside her. Suddenly she felt like the spoils of war.

'You've really given up the idea of building a resort here?' she asked in a subdued voice.

'Kaoga Bay will survive without it,' he said. Surprisingly, he didn't sound too upset about it. 'People come here wanting a simple, relaxed lifestyle. They'll still be able to find that. Maybe that's what I need too—an easier, more relaxed way of life.' He touched her cheek with his hand. 'As long as you're here to enjoy it with me.'

She felt her heart skip a beat, but caution prevented her from getting too excited. Was he talking days? Weeks? Months? And what would happen after he'd taken his relaxing break with her? Would he go back to his high-pressured life in Sydney? And say goodbye?

'You want me to stay down here for a bit longer?' she asked carefully. 'While you oversee the repairs to Harry's house?'

'I won't need to stay down here while the repairs are being done,' he said. 'I'll have experts to look after all that. In a day or two I'll be going back to Sydney. I've come to a decision.'

Her mouth went dry. *That* was his idea of a relaxing break? A *day* or two?

'A decision?' she echoed in a hoarse whisper.

His hand stroked down her cheek, across her jaw, lightly fingering the cleft in her chin. 'I'm getting out of the property development business. I'm going back to designing, Sandra ... architecture.

'The first thing I intend to do is design a fun park for this headland ... for young kids. On the land behind my house and Harry's. It was what I had in mind when my son was born, but I scrubbed it when he ... died. Just as I scrubbed a lot of the ideals and values I used to live by.' But his voice was no longer bitter, and the harshness was gone.

'Trent, I'm so pleased. It's a wonderful idea,' she cried. She tilted her head at him. 'What do you mean...*behind* your house?' she asked slowly. 'You're saying——'

'I'm saying I've decided against demolishing this place.' He smiled suddenly. 'I think I might have some use for a holiday home after all. I might even set up a permanent office here, so I can work down here if I want to.' He gave a low chuckle. 'Magda will be happy; she can go on living here, looking after the place for me. I'll find someone from the town to do any heavy work, and the garden.'

She gulped. 'Well, you have it all worked out.' She smiled back at him a trifle shakily. 'So you'll be leaving Kaoga Bay in the next couple of days?'

She would go back to Sydney too, she decided, even though she wasn't due back at work for another couple of weeks. She would go back to her small flat in the suburbs and hope that Trent would want to see more of her once they were both back in town. Would he? Once he was back there, busy closing doors on one career and launching another?

'Give or take a day.' His hand slid round her neck, his face blurring over hers as he touched her lips with his, lightly, tantalisingly, once, twice, three times. 'Sandra, I want you to come back with me.'

With him? What did he mean, *with*? 'You'd like to go on seeing me in Sydney?' she breathed, wondering in quick panic if it would be wise to go on seeing him at all, feeling the way she did about him. Surely she'd be a fool to get more deeply involved, not knowing how long it would last, knowing he didn't love her, knowing he would never love another woman the way he had loved his wife, Celia...would never allow himself to be that vulnerable again.

'Not just see you, Sandra. Be with you. Have you with me. I want us to be together.'

Her lips parted. '*Together*, Trent?' She eyed him warily, needing all her strength to hold back the hope that tugged at her insides.

'I'm not talking about an affair, Sandra, a passing fling,' he said quietly. 'I don't want you with me for just a few weeks, or months. I want you to be a part of my life. Now and... always.'

The room seemed to tilt and slowly roll over. 'Trent, what are you saying?' she asked huskily. 'That you want me to come and *live* with you?'

'Of course I'll want you living with me.' He gave an impatient twitch of his shoulder. 'How else would you be with me for always?'

She gulped. 'As your... lover, you mean?'

'Lover, companion, friend, life partner...' He pressed his mouth to hers, muffling the words against the softness of her lips. Then he drew back, just far enough to say, his words startling her, unbelievable to her ears, 'Sandra, I love you.' His eyes were scorchingly tender. 'I'm not going to hold back the way I feel or what I want from you because I know nothing's going to change the way I feel now. When I love...'

He paused, and she sensed the strong emotion affecting him, making it difficult for him to put his feelings into words. 'Sandra, I've never been more sure of anything in my life.' He spoke with an intensity that seemed to come from deep down inside him. 'I love you and I never want to be without you. Now or ever. I think... hope... you're beginning to feel the same. Tell me I'm not wrong!' Naked emotion darkened the eyes impaling hers.

She shook her head and swallowed. 'You're not wrong,' she breathed, and dragged in a tremulous sigh, holding back—for the moment at least—any further admissions. 'And you... you want me to come and live with you?'

'Not just *live* with me, damn it! Be my...' He sucked in an impatient breath, and she thought, with a tightening in her throat, You still can't say it, can you? The shadows of the past are still holding you back, keeping a part of you from me, preventing you from grabbing hold of what you want.

He seemed to read what was in her eyes. 'For pity's sake, Sandra, you know what I'm going to want from you. *Marriage*! I'm asking you to *marry* me!'

A deep quiver of sheer happiness rippled through her. But she curbed it to ask steadily, 'You mean you want me to be your...?' She paused deliberately. She was going to make him say it if it killed her!

'My *wife*, damn it! I want you to be my wife! What else would you be if I married you?'

She smiled sweetly up at him. 'I just wanted to be sure that *you* knew. That it was what *you* wanted. A wife. That's what I would be, Trent, if I married you. Your wife. Your second wife,' she said deliberately.

'Ah,' he said as light dawned at last. 'Sandra, my darling, I promise you, I swear to you, it wasn't the thought of Celia...the memory of Celia...that held me back. It's... I don't know. Fear. Apprehension. Of letting you down the way I...' A silver flame blazed in his eyes. His voice was hoarse as he explained, 'It's because you've become so damned precious to me already that I couldn't bear the thought of losing you...too.'

She gulped down the lump that rose to her throat. 'I'm pretty tough, you know,' she assured him huskily. 'I'm my father's daughter. Harry's taught me that if you want something enough—happiness, whatever—you must grab it while the chance is there. Otherwise you might miss out. Any happiness, no matter how brief, is better, surely, than no happiness at all.'

His eyes locked with hers. 'It's taken me a long time to see that,' he said. 'To be able to look back without a black wall of guilt and self-blame standing in the way,

blocking out the memories, both good and bad. It's taken you to show me how...'

She tried to answer lightly, to cover the flare of emotion that swelled inside her. 'It took me a while too...to realise you weren't as cold and unfeeling as you made out, that you were trying to hide the human, caring side of you because you saw it as a weakness, a weakness that could make you vulnerable, and capable of being hurt again.'

His voice throbbed out of the brief silence that followed. 'Knowing that someone knows me so well,' he murmured, his hand stroking down her cheek, 'makes me feel very vulnerable indeed.'

She smiled and shook her head. 'You're the strongest man I know. But you won't need to be strong *alone* any more. You'll have me. We'll have each other. I love you, Trent.' Just being in his arms made her feel as if she had everything in life that she wanted, or would ever need.

'You give me more than I deserve,' he said thickly. 'What do I have that I can offer you? I know that money, possessions, material things, are not what you want from me.'

'Give me your love, Trent,' she whispered. 'And your goodness, your loyalty, your strength... They're all I'll ever want. Except maybe children, one day. Our children.'

She saw a pulse jump at his temple. He didn't say a word, but the emotion in his eyes as he brought his mouth down on hers told her everything she needed to know.

MILLS & BOON

Just Married

Celebrate the joy, excitement and adjustment that comes with being 'Just Married' in this wonderful collection of four new short stories.

Written by four popular authors

Sandra Canfield

Muriel Jensen

Elise Title

Rebecca Winters

Just Married is guaranteed to melt your hearts— just married or not!

Available: April 1996   Price: £4.99

Temptation

Coming up in
BACHELOR ARMS...

When Blythe Fielding planned her wedding and asked her two best friends, Caitlin and Lily, to be bridesmaids, none of them had a clue a new romance was around the corner for each of them—even the bride!

These entertaining, dramatic stories of friendship, mystery and love by **JoAnn Ross** continue to follow the exploits of the residents of Bachelor Arms. If you loved the male Bachelor Arms titles you'll love the next set coming up in Temptation featuring the female residents of this lively apartment block.

Look out for:

FOR RICHER OR POORER (March 1996)
THREE GROOMS AND A WEDDING (April 1996)

GET 4 BOOKS AND A MYSTERY GIFT

Return this coupon and we'll send you 4 Mills & Boon Romances and a mystery gift absolutely FREE! We'll even pay the postage and packing for you.

We're making you this offer to introduce you to the benefits of Reader Service: FREE home delivery of brand-new Mills & Boon romances, at least a month before they are available in the shops, FREE gifts and a monthly Newsletter packed with information.

Accepting these FREE books and gift places you under no obligation to buy, you may cancel at any time, even after receiving just your free shipment. Simply complete the coupon below and send it to:

MILLS & BOON READER SERVICE, FREEPOST, CROYDON, SURREY, CR9 3WZ.

No stamp needed

Yes, please send me 4 free Mills & Boon Romances and a mystery gift. I understand that unless you hear from me, I will receive 6 superb new titles every month for just £2.10* each postage and packing free. I am under no obligation to purchase any books and I may cancel or suspend my subscription at any time, but the free books and gifts will be mine to keep in any case. (I am over 18 years of age)

1EP6R

Ms/Mrs/Miss/Mr _____

Address _____

_____

_____ Postcode _____

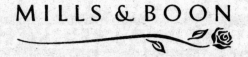

MILLS & BOON

Next Month's Romances

Each month you can choose from a wide variety of romance with Mills & Boon. Below are the new titles to look out for next month.

HOT BLOOD	Charlotte Lamb
PRISONER OF PASSION	Lynne Graham
A WIFE IN WAITING	Jessica Steele
A WOMAN TO REMEMBER	Miranda Lee
SPRING BRIDE	Sandra Marton
DESPERATELY SEEKING ANNIE	Patricia Knoll
THE BACHELOR CHASE	Emma Richmond
TAMING A TYCOON	Leigh Michaels
PASSION WITH INTENT	Natalie Fox
RUTHLESS!	Lee Wilkinson
MY HERO	Debbie Macomber
UNDERCOVER LOVER	Heather Allison
REBEL BRIDE	Sally Carr
SECRET COURTSHIP	Grace Green
PERFECT STRANGERS	Laura Martin
HEART'S REFUGE	Quinn Wilder